HAUNTED REVELATIONS: A TALE OF DECEPTION

# OrangeBooks Publication

1st Floor, Rajhans Arcade, Mall Road, Kohka, Bhilai, Chhattisgarh 490020

Website: **www.orangebooks.in**

---

**© Copyright, 2024, Author**

All rights reserved. No part of this book may be reproduced, stored in a retrieval system, or transmitted, in any form by any means, electronic, mechanical, magnetic, optical, chemical, manual, photocopying, recording or otherwise, without the prior written consent of its writer.

**First Edition, 2024**
**ISBN:** 978-93-6554-026-0

# HAUNTED REVELATIONS: A TALE OF DECEPTION

A SUSPENSEFUL
JOURNEY INTO THE
HEART OF DECEIT

## Dr.Shubhada Chourishi

OrangeBooks Publication
www.orangebooks.in

# Acknowledgement

I am deeply grateful to everyone who has been a part of my journey and supported me in bringing this book to life. Firstly, I want to express my heartfelt gratitude to my grandfather, Mr. Purushottam Chourishi, whose unwavering belief in me has been a constant source of inspiration.

To my parents, Dr. Shailendra Chourishi and Mrs. Uma Chourishi, your endless encouragement and persistent support have been my guiding light through every phase of my life. You have always been there, holding my hand with love and understanding.

My brother and sister-in-law, Dr. Shubham and Archi, you have been my pillars of strength and my partners in crime, always there with a listening ear and a helping hand. Thank you to my sister Vaishanavi Chourasia for all the love and support you have shown me, and for being my all-time favourite critic, teaching me about new-generation technology.

To my in-laws, Mr. Dinesh Sharma, Mrs. Avanta Sharma, Mr. Saurabh Sharma, and Puja Sharma, thank you for welcoming me into your family with open arms and showering me with love and support.

Special thanks to my favourite uncle, Mr. Rajeev Mishra, whose cheerful presence and invaluable assistance have meant the world to me.

A heartfelt thank you to my dear friend, Mr. Bilal Ahmed Khan, who not only believed in me but also encouraged me to discover the author within myself. Your relentless support has been a beacon of strength.

To all my friends—Nabila, Kamlesh, Smrutiprasad Paikaray, Purushottam P, Dr. Rujuta, Siyona, Abhash, Sonali, Vasu, Ayush & Yash—your love and care have filled my life with warmth and joy. I cherish each of you for being a part of my journey. Thank you to my BEST FRIEND, Dr. Ankit Chakravarti, who is the true definition of a friend. Your unwavering support through all my failures and your patience in handling my tantrums, no matter what, has been invaluable.

I am incredibly blessed to have the most wonderful husband, Mr. Rishabh Sharma by my side. Your persistent support, boundless love, and infectious optimism have been my rock. You have cheered me on through every challenge, celebrated every success, and made every moment of life, an adventure. Your belief in me is my greatest strength, and I am proud to call you my partner. You truly are the epitome of the perfect partner that every woman dreams of.

To my two newborn nieces, Sonayra and Dityaa, who have brought immense joy into my life—thank you for making my life complete.

Saved the BEST for the LAST- Thank you so much my two beloved furr babies, Fluffy and Caesar, who have taught me the true meaning of unconditional love and made me a better person with their companionship and devotion—you are the best things in my world.

**I must thank myself for believing in myself! Through every challenge and triumph, I've been my own cheerleader, and for that, I am truly proud.**

# Preface

In the intricate dance of life, we all wear masks. We project an image of perfection, shielding our vulnerabilities from the world. But what happens when the facade begins to crack, and the truth threatens to surface? "Haunted Revelations: A Tale of Deception" delves into the complexities of human nature, exploring the delicate balance between appearance and reality.

This story centers around Sayesha, a woman whose life appears enviable from the outside. With professional success and a close-knit group of friends, she seems to have it all. Yet, beneath this veneer lies a world of secrets and hidden fears. As Sayesha navigates the choppy waters of deception and revelation, she must confront not only the external threats that haunt her but also the internal demons she has long suppressed.

The journey within these pages is one of suspense and intrigue, where every twist and turn unravels a new layer of mystery. Through vivid descriptions and engaging dialogue, the narrative invites you to step into Sayesha's world, to experience her triumphs and tribulations, and to question the very nature of truth and illusion.

"Haunted Revelations: A Tale of Deception" is more than just a story of suspense; it is a reflection on the human condition, on the secrets we keep, and the courage it takes to face them. As you turn the pages, may you find yourself drawn into the labyrinth of Sayesha's life, and perhaps, discover a few revelations of your own.

# Content

Acknowledgement..................................................................iv

Preface ..............................................................................vii

**Chapter - 1**
The Perfect Life......................................................................1

**Chapter - 2**
Secrets Unraveled ...............................................................17

**Chapter - 3**
Ishan's Dark Discovery........................................................40

**Chapter - 4**
The Hidden Fear .................................................................46

**Chapter - 5**
The Forbidden Ritual ..........................................................58

**Chapter - 6**
The Haunted Confrontation ...............................................67

**Chapter - 7**
Hari's Skullduggery.............................................................83

**Chapter - 8**
　　Secrets And Lies ................................................................. 95

**Chapter - 9**
　　From Greed To Death ..................................................... 114

**AUTHOR'S BIO** ................................................................. **143**

## Chapter - 1
# THE PERFECT LIFE

A small-town girl, Sayesha, was sitting on a bench in the park, enjoying her solitude. It was July 24th, 2009, a beautiful day with cloudy skies and a cold breeze rustling through the leaves of the graceful Gulmohar trees. The birds were chirping, and she noticed a mamma bird sheltering her babies with her wings, protecting them from the cool weather. The scene was so mesmerizing that Sayesha lost herself in the beauty of her surroundings, completely forgetting she had planned a party at her place today. All her childhood friends were invited.

Sayesha, or Sash as her friends called her, was a well-known architect and interior designer. Her presence was as impressive as the buildings she designed. She had this way of seeing beauty and functionality in spaces that others couldn't. Whether she was in professional attire or chilling out, you could tell she had an eye for creating spaces that were both stunning and practical. Sayesha's smile and the way she talked about her work showed her passion for pushing boundaries in architecture and making dreams come alive in her designs.

She had designed approximately 127 buildings, transforming them into beautiful homes. Successful and wealthy, she was married to Raj, a handsome financial advisor. Sayesha had many friends who adored her for her helpful nature and kindness. She embodied everything anyone aspired to be. Her life seemed perfect, and everyone wished they could be like Sayesha.

As mid-evening approached, she reluctantly got up from the bench, remembering she needed to cook dinner for her friends. She couldn't be happier, knowing she was about to reunite with her childhood friends after such a long time.

She had a circle of five friends including herself.

Nisha, a sharp Chartered Accountant, had this vibe of being smart with numbers. She just knew her stuff, and her eyes were like they could see right through financial puzzles. Always dressed sharp, like she meant business, you could tell she was all about precision and getting things right in the financial world.

Ava, a fashion designer, was like a walking rainbow. Her style was all about creativity and mixing things up. Whether it was on the runway or just hanging out, Ava's clothes were a total expression of her artsy side. You could see her passion for making people feel unique and confident in what they wore.

Kush, a theatre guy, was all drama and charm. On stage or off, he had this way of drawing you in with his stories and emotions. His clothes mirrored the characters he played—full of personality and depth. You could spot him in a crowd just by his theatrical presence and how he carried himself.

Ishan, a stock market guru, was the guy who knew where the money was at. Always dressed sharp, like he belonged in the financial district, he had this quiet confidence about him. Ishan could read trends and opportunities like it was second nature, and you could see he knew his way around the world of finance.

**Ding Dong...**

**Sash:** *[Rushing in from another room]* Coming!

**Nisha:** *[Hugging Sash]* Hi, my love. How are you doing? Oh my god, look at you in that kitchen apron. It suits you well.

**Sash:** *[Laughing softly]* Hehe he... I'm good, and since I'm beautiful, I look good in everything.

**Ishan:** *[Grumbling as he enters]* Move aside. Did you really have to have the party tonight? There's an important match today.

**Sash:** Today? In this rainy weather?

**Ishan:** *[Turning on the TV and ignoring her]* Shh... Let me listen to the commentary.

**Sash:** *[Turning back]* Hey Kush! How are you, my love?

**Kush:** *[Entering with a tired smile]* I'm good but works got me stuck these days. It's been hectic.

**Nisha:** I smell something burning.

**Sash:** *[Eyes widening]* Oh no, it's my chicken curry!

**Ava:** *[Calmly walking in]* Chill, I switched off the gas.

**Sash:** Thank God. How are you doing, Ava?

Ava looked at Sayesha for a few seconds and took a deep breath.

**Ava:** *[With a weary sigh]* My life is stuck in a loop too. Even though I work from home, there are so many household chores to do, and of course, I have to take care of my kid. I'm exhausted.

**Sash:** Hire a maid, madam.

**Ava:** *[Frustrated]* I have, but she takes too many leaves. We're not as lucky as you, Sash. I wish I could have a life like yours—a successful architect, a rich husband, a happy life, and of course, a good maid. You look pretty, your life is smooth without any restrictions or responsibilities. *[Making a sad face, almost pleading]*

God, please make my life just like Sash's. Please, God. Please!

**Sash:** *[Comforting]* Relax, madam. Chill! Everything is going to be okay. You just need some time. It will heal everything. Take a break, trust God, and remember you have a friend like me. You should be happy.

**Nisha & Kush :** *[together, in agreement]* Ava is right.

**Nisha:** We all need a life like yours, Sash. Of course, we're not jealous; we're very happy for you, but we need a life just like yours.

**Kush:** *[Changing the subject]* Okay, enough. Where is Raj?

**Sash:** He went to an office party with his colleagues. So, it's just us today.

**Ishan:** *[Annoyed, trying to focus on the TV]* Can you guys just shut up? I'm trying to watch something.

**Sash:** *[Scolding gently]* Ishan don't be so rude. Don't behave like a kid. Just go to my room and watch TV in peace there. I'll call you when dinner's ready.

**Ishan:** Fine, bye.

Ishan switched off the TV and went to Sayesha's bedroom. He was looking for the remote.

**Ishan** *[shouting, frustrated]* Sash! Where is the stupid remote?

**Sash:** *[Sighing]* He is still a child. Coming!

Sayesha went to the bedroom and searched for the remote. She was tossing and turning her pillows when Ishan saw something strange and was shocked.

**Sash:** *[Handing him the remote, teasing]* Here. It was lying on the dressing table. You have two big eyes, don't you? Now take this remote and watch your stupid match.

**Ishan:** *[Grateful, trying to mask his curiosity]* Thanks, sweetheart.

When Sayesha went back, Ishan closed the bedroom door and looked under her pillow. He saw three knives lying there. He was curious and disturbed after seeing them.

**Ishan** *[to himself]*: Sorry, Sash, I need to find out what's going on.

He looked over her books, her cupboard, and her clothes. When he opened her cupboard, he found a napkin stained with blood. Then, he searched her dressing table and found lots of tablets. He was confused. After some time, his eyes caught a shimmery notebook lying in the corner of the room, covered with a cloth. He opened it and read many confessions that Sayesha had written. He was even more confused now, trying to figure out the story behind all of this. He just knew that Sayesha was not happy.

Then he tried to switch off the TV, but the remote stopped working, so he thought of turning it off from the main switch behind the TV. The moment he went there, he saw many pages stapled together. He pulled them out and found threat notes. Some of them said:

"My mom was right."

- "K.N.I.F.E"
- "M.I.S.S. Y.O.U"

He got scared and was curious to know what was going on. Ishan unlocked the door and saw Sayesha laughing like a child.

**Sash** *[talking to her friends, giggling]* And you remember that day we were caught eating chocolates in our classroom.

All her friends were laughing, and Ishan just realized that Sayesha was the most mature among them. She knew how to hide her pain so well behind that laughter. He kept observing her, only to find out that she wanted the child inside her to be free and happy, but she could not, contrary to what everyone thought.

Ishan was standing so quietly in the corner that nobody saw him. Suddenly, Ava felt a shadow behind her and turned around.

**Ava:** *[Startled]* Ishan??? You scared me. Is your match over?

**Ishan:** No, I just don't feel like watching anymore. You all are enjoying yourselves here, so why should I miss these interesting conversations?

**Nisha:** *[Smiling]* He and his mood swings. Come and sit with us. We're playing Snake and Ladders like old times.

**Sash:** You guys start the next game. I'll just check if the chicken is cooked and be with you in 5 minutes.

**Ishan:** Come, I'll help you in the kitchen.

**Sash:** It's okay. I've got it, Babe.

Ishan still went to the kitchen and started talking to Sayesha while she was adding spices to the curry.

**Ishan:** *[Observing her closely]* You're looking cute today, Sash. You've achieved everything you ever dreamt of. In the race of life, you're at the top, just like in high school.

**Sash:** Of course, Ishan. I am the best.

**Ishan:** *[Softly]* Are you happy?

**Sash:** *[Overly cheerful]* Of course, I am. I'm the happiest person on this planet. Touch wood, I've received everything I ever wanted. Haven't you heard? People want to live my life, MY LIFE ... Ok, enough of this chat. Let's go and play your favourite game.

**Ishan:** *[Surprised]* You still remember?

**Sash:** *[Smiling]* Of course I do. That's one of my good qualities—I don't forget.

Sayesha turned around, and Ishan caught her hand, pulling her towards him with one hand holding her wrist tightly and the other on her waist.

**Sash:** *[Alarmed]* What the hell are you doing?

**Ishan:** *[Demanding]* If you're happy, Sash, then what are these marks on your hand? Why are there knives under your pillow? Why is your journal full of confessions? What are those threatening notes?

**Sash:** *[With tears in her eyes, defensive]* Who are you to ask me such questions?

**Ishan:** *[Firmly]* Tell me the truth.

**Sash:** *[In pain]* Ishan. It's hurting. Leave me.

**Ishan:** No.

**Sash:** *[Sighing]* Fine, listen. I fell in my kitchen yesterday and hit the sharp edge of that stupid broken bucket, so I have these scars. I get bad dreams, hence the knives under my pillow, and everyone has confessions. I just keep a journal. *[Irritated]* You shouldn't have violated my privacy by checking my room and reading my journal. Now leave my hand, you're hurting me, Ishan.

**Ishan:** *[Asking softly but insistently]* What about the notes? I won't let go until I know the truth.

**Sash:** *[Exasperated]* This is the truth.

**Ishan:** What about the notes, Sash?

Sayesha remained silent; her gaze fixed on the floor. Ishan repeated his question, his tone firmer this time.

**Nisha:** *[Concerned, peering into the room]* Sash!! Ishan!! Is everything okay?

**Ishan:** *[Trying to sound casual, though his worry is evident]* Yes, everything is fine. We were just having a conversation.

**Nisha:** Alright then. The second round of the game is about to start. Are you both joining us, or should I come and fetch you?

**Ishan:** Yes, we're coming. *[Turning to Sayesha, his voice gentle but insistent]* What are those threat notes, Sash?

Sayesha had tears in her eyes, and it felt as if she was guilty. Ishan removed his hand from her waist and wrist, when he saw her eyes. He had known Sayesha since childhood and had always seen her laugh. He had never imagined that she could also weep.

Both of them made their way to the living room, joining others for the game.

As they played, Ishan's mind wandered, troubled. He had always seen Sayesha as the ever- smiling, dependable friend—someone who was always there with a solution. No one had ever seen her cry before. In his introspection, he realized that perhaps they had overlooked her humanity. She had always been the one to support others, never showing her own vulnerabilities.

**Ishan:** *[Musing to himself, conflicted]* But could she be hiding something? Have we misjudged her all these years? Is there a darker side to her that we've never seen?

**Ava:** *[Calling out, a hint of impatience]* Ishan! Ishan! Ishan!

**Ishan:** *[Startled, snapping out of his thoughts]* Huh?

**Ava:** What are you thinking about? Roll the dice, dude.

**Ishan:** *[Rolling the dice with a grin]* I'm going to win this game for sure, just like old times.

**Kush:** *[Teasing, with a smirk]* Let's see. I think Sash has a winning streak everywhere, not you.

**Sash:** I want Ishan to win this time.

Ishan glanced at Sayesha, noticing a silent plea in her eyes. It seemed as though she wanted to say something, her gaze revealing the depth of her inner turmoil. He sensed that she wasn't guilty but deeply disturbed.

**Kush:** *[Raising an eyebrow, curious]* Really? You want him to win? What's going on with you?

**Ishan:** *[Jokingly, trying to deflect the tension]* She's in love with me, obviously. Right, Sash?

**Sash:** *[With a teasing smile]* In your dreams, babe.

Finally, Ishan won the game. Sayesha let out a sigh, as if she had deliberately wanted him to win. Her eyes met his with a glimmer of hope, leaving Ishan puzzled about her true intentions. It felt like there was something more she wasn't saying, something she might be deliberately hinting at.

**Tring! Tring!**

**Ava:** *[Answering the phone, her voice soft and tender]* Hello... Hmm... Yes, baby, Mumma is at Masi's place.

Have you finished your homework? Baby, Mumma will be home in an hour. Go to sleep without me tonight, and I'll make your favourite breakfast in the morning. Yes... Yes... Yes... Sure. Good night, my love.

**Ava:** *[Exhaling deeply, visibly relieved]* Phew... This kid is going to kill me. Can we have dinner now, please? I'm starving. Sash, is dinner ready?

**Sash:** Yes, dinner is ready. Give me five minutes, and I'll serve it.

**Nisha:** *[With a touch of impatience]* We're not kids anymore. We can serve ourselves.

**Sash:** *[Smiling, conceding]* Okay, but let me just put it on the dining table.

**Ava:** Come on, I'll help you.

**Kush:** You sit, madam. I'll help her.

**Ava:** *[Gratefully]* Thank you, Kush. You're a darling. I'm so exhausted today.

Kush and Sayesha reheated the food while Nisha set up the dining table. They brought the food out and were about to serve it.

**Nisha:** *[With a playful grin]* Again, we're not kids. We'll serve ourselves.

They all enjoyed the delicious Indian dinner prepared by Sayesha.

**Ava:** *[Savouring the food]* Sash, this chicken curry is fabulous. I need the recipe, babe.

**Nisha:** *[Impressed]* I usually don't eat chicken that much, but this is pure bliss.

**Kush:** Sash is amazing at everything, whatever the task.

**Ishan:** *[Noticing Sayesha's lack of appetite]* Why aren't you eating, Sash?

**Sash:** *[With a nonchalant shrug]* Oh, I had a late lunch, and after all this cooking, I don't feel like eating. I'll have some later.

**Ava:** *[Concerned]* Eat something at least. It's already 11 p.m. When will you eat then?

**Sash:** *[Reluctantly]* Fine, I'll have some salad and rice.

They all settled in the living room, exhausted but content. It was time for dessert.

**Sash:** *[Cheerfully]* Anyone up for ice cream?

**Ishan:** *[Curiously]* Depends. What flavours do you have?

**Sash:** *[Enthusiastically]* Well, I have chocolate, vanilla, and strawberry.

**Nisha:** I'll have a scoop of chocolate and one scoop of vanilla.

**Ava:** Two scoops of strawberry, please.

**Kush:** I want only one scoop of vanilla.

**Ishan:** *[Sweetly]* Let's go, Sash. I'll help you serve the ice cream.

They both went into the kitchen. Ishan got the ice cream cups while Sayesha retrieved the ice cream from the freezer.

**Ishan:** *[Firmly, yet kindly]* Sash, you know I won't let go until you tell me the truth.

**Sash:** *[With a touch of frustration]* Ishan, some things are personal. Let it be that way.

**Ishan:** *[biting his teeth, irritated]* I don't interfere in someone's personal affairs unless it's harming them. I can see you're not okay. I just want to know if there's any way, I can help you get through this.

**Sash:** *[Softly, redirecting the conversation]* We'll talk about it later. Let's first take these ice creams outside before they melt.

**Ishan:** Okay.

**Sash:** *[Handing out the ice cream cups]* Here you go, guys. Please take your ice cream cups.

**Nisha:** Thank you, Sash.

**Ava:** *[Curiously]* Sash, remember you mentioned a shop near CSH College where one can find delightful beachwear?

**Sash:** *[Nodding]* Ah yes, the "Pisces Wonderland" store, indeed.

**Ava:** Perfect! I'm planning a trip to Bali with my college friends. Could you accompany me to that shop?

**Kush:** *[Feigning surprise and being dramatic]* And you haven't mentioned this to us yet? Astonishing!

**Ava:** It was only decided yesterday.

**Sash:** *[Reassuringly]* It's perfectly fine. I'll join you at the store, the day after tomorrow evening. No need to worry.

**Ava:** I love you, sweetheart. Thank you so much.

**Ishan:** I'm feeling very sleepy. I think I'll leave now.

**Kush:** *[Curiously]* Wait, did you bring your car?

**Ishan:** Yes.

**Kush:** Drop Nisha and me off too.

**Ishan:** *[Turning towards Ava]* What about you, Ava?

**Ava:** *[Smiling]* Oh, I brought my own car. *[Turning towards Kush & Nisha]* Since both your homes are on my route, I'll drop you off. Ishan, no need to worry about it.

**Kush:** *[Relieved]* Great!

**Ishan:** *[Gratefully]* Sash, thank you for this evening. We had a wonderful time.

**Nisha:** It's been such a long time since we've gathered. I don't want to leave, but duty calls tomorrow.

**Sash:** *[Warmly]* It was truly wonderful to see you all. We'll meet again soon. I promise to make time for our reunions.

**Nisha:** Yes, Sash. Take care and convey our regards to Raj.

**Kush:** *[Teasingly]* Goodbye, Sash. Dinner was delightful, but perhaps you should learn more about how to cook. Lolz.

*[Sayesha pinches Kush playfully, and they share a laugh]*

**Ava:** *[Firmly]* Sash, remember our shopping date, day after tomorrow. No backing out this time.

**Sash:** *[Assuredly]* Absolutely, darling. See you at 5 p.m. *[Turning towards Ishan]* Ishaan? You seem awfully quiet. What's on your mind?

**Ishan:** Nothing much, just feeling a bit nauseated from the undercooked chicken you served.

**Sash:** *[Playfully annoyed]* I will give you a tight slap. You're such an idiot.

Sayesha then hugged Ishan, and he whispered, "I want to know everything." She didn't utter a word.

## Chapter - 2
## SECRETS UNRAVELED

Everyone left, and when Sayesha looked at the clock, it was 1 a.m. She went to take a shower, thinking about what Ishan had said. Some questions were stuck in her mind:

*[**Sash** (thinking): Why is he so worried about me? How does he know something's wrong? How did he find the knives? I should have been more careful with my stuff. I won't tell him anything. Isn't it what I wanted?].*

She came out of the shower, dressed up, and was preparing her bed when she heard the doorbell.

*[Sash (to herself): He comes directly; he never rings the bell.]*

She went to the living room and tried to look through the peephole, but no one was there. She partly opened the door only to realize it was Ishan standing outside.

**Sash:** *[Startled]* What the hell, Ishan? You scared me. What do you need?

**Ishan:** *[Calmly]* Can I please come inside first?

Sayesha opened the door, and Ishan came in and sat on the couch. He instructed her to close the door. She knew what was going to happen, so she rolled her eyes and closed the door.

**Tring... Tring...**

Sayesha picked up the call. It was Raj. He informed her that he would be coming late as one of his colleagues had an accident and they were taking him to the hospital.

**Ishan:** *[Sincerely]* That's great. Just you and me then.

**Sash:** *[Irritated]* What do you want, Ishan?

**Ishan:** *[Earnestly]* You know very well what I want. I need to know the truth, Sash. We've been friends for a long time, even though we haven't interacted much. But now I'm concerned about you. You haven't told anyone what's going on. Please tell me.

**Sash:** *[Defensively]* I'm very happy, Ishan. I'm living my dream life. There's nothing wrong. I'm perfect. I have a beautiful family, a good job, a happy life, a nice house...

Ishan immediately pulled her close and hugged her tightly as she spoke. Sayesha felt warm and comfortable. She felt safe. Tears rolled down her eyes. She wanted to say a lot, but words were stuck in her mouth.

**Ishan:** *[Soothingly]* Shhh... Shhh... Shhh... I don't need to know anything, okay? I just want you to know that I'm here.

She hugged him tighter. No questions, no answers, just a friend close to her heart. There was silence, and the only sound heard was the clock ticking. They hugged each other for a very long time. His t-shirt was almost wet with Sayesha's tears. One hand was on her waist, the other on the back of her head, and she clung to him like a baby kangaroo. She hadn't felt so relaxed in a long time.

**Ishan:** *[Light-heartedly]* Do you have a good detergent?

**Sash:** *[Confused]* Why?

**Ishan:** *[Playfully]* I need to get your lipstick stain off my t-shirt, or people will think something stupid happened.

Sayesha moved away resting her head on his shoulder but finally smiled, and this time it was NOT a fake smile. She took a deep breath and asked Ishan if he wanted coffee. He replied:

**Ishan:** I'll make it for both of us. Black, no sugar, no cream, right?

**Sash:** *[Surprised]* You remember?

**Ishan:** *[Repeating Sayesha's earlier words, mimicking her voice]* Of course I do. This is another good thing about me. I don't forget.

**Sash:** *[Laughing]* Hahaha.

She nodded yes. He made coffee, and then they sat on the couch.

**Ishan:** *[Concerned]* Seriously, Sash! I've never seen you so weak. Is there anything I can do to help you?

**Sash:** *[Solemnly]* No, Ishan, no one can do anything. I want to tell you everything, but I'm not sure what you'll think of me.

**Ishan:** *[Reassuringly]* Sash, as I told you earlier, we haven't been that close, but trust me, I won't judge you ever.

There was silence for a few minutes while Sayesha sipped her coffee. She felt a mix of fear and comfort. She knew Ishan was there to help her, but she wasn't sure if she was ready to tell him the big truth. Ishan continuously stared at Sayesha, trying to understand what was going on with her. Sayesha thought for some time and decided to tell Ishan the truth.

**Sash:** There is no Raj.

**Ishan:** What?? No Raj? What do you mean?

**Sash:** Have you ever met Raj?

**Ishan:** Yes, at your wedding.

**Sash:** *[Challenging]* What wedding? I got married in court, remember?

**Ishan:** *[Trying to recall]* Yes, but you met all of us in the evening around 5:30 p.m on the day of your marriage. We have pictures too. We met Raj. We talked to him.

**Sash:** Ishan, what the hell? You're scaring the hell out of me. We never met after I got married.

**Ishan:** *[Insisting]* Do you remember we met at Ava's Lake house in the evening?

**Sash:** *[Firmly]* Ishan? Ava's lake house is on the Konkan side, and it takes around 6-7 hours to get there. As long as I remember, I got married around 2 p.m and we did a conference call around 3:30 p.m., and you're saying we all met at Ava's Lake house around 5:30 p.m.?

**Ishan:** *[Confused]* How is that possible, Sash? Maybe I'm getting the details wrong. Maybe we met the next day.

**Sash:** Ishan, the next day I went to an award ceremony in Alibaug. You all couldn't come because you were at Ava's Lake house.

**Ishan:** *[Frustrated]* My head is hurting now, Sash. Tell me the whole story. Did you or did you not get married?

**Sash:** Yes, I did, but no, I did not.

**Ishan:** *[Bewildered]* What do you mean by that, and who is this, Raj?

**Sash:** Do you remember my uncle, Shastri?

**Ishan:** *[Nodding]* Yes, he passed away a few years ago.

**Sash:** *[Sorrowfully]* Yes. So, he had leukaemia and was on his deathbed in February 2007. He loved me so much. The doctors told us he had very few days to live. He said he would love to see me married before he died. My whole family was shocked at how we would find a good man for me in such a short amount of time. Suddenly, my little sister Prachi had a stupid plan.

**Sash** *[speaking in Prachi's voice]*: "Di, what if we take a random boy to the hospital and tell him that he's the one Sash married in court today because we didn't have time for a big wedding?"

**Ishan:** *[Confused]* You should have asked any of us to marry you if it was fake. Who is this, Raj?

**Sash:** Why? You couldn't have married me for real?

**Ishan:** *[Serious]* This isn't a joke, Sash. Tell me who Raj is and what happened next.

**Sash:** Okay, so my dad didn't agree at first, but when Kaka insisted a lot, he said fine, we'll go with Prachi's plan.

**Ishan:** *[Curious]* Then?

**Sash:** We were wondering which boy to ask. Then, while we were exiting the hospital, we saw a very handsome boy named Sarthak sitting on a bench in the hospital's garden premises.

**Ishan:** *[Confused]* That hospital doesn't have a garden.

**Sash:** *[Softly, trying to get her thoughts together]* I know, but listen to me first. My father saw him and couldn't stop himself from asking what happened. Sarthak said, "I don't have anyone with me. I am all alone," and started crying. *[Pause, looking away]* My dad felt bad for him and offered him a job in his company along with 10 lakh rupees if he would agree to act as if he was marrying me for my uncle's sake.

*[Slight smile, lost in memory]* Sarthak seemed to have a glow in his personality. He was tall with black eyes, long hair, a muscular build, and I couldn't take my eyes off him. He looked at me, and I have no idea what he thought, but he got up from the bench, looked into my eyes, and smiled, saying, "I will marry her."

*[More animated, gesturing with her hands]* My dad said, "You don't have to marry her in real life. You just have to act in front of her uncle." Sarthak said, "OKAY." We took him to my uncle's room and told him he is the man I am getting married to. Kaka was very happy and asked him his name. He said "Raj."

*[Laughing softly]* We were all shocked, but later he told us he wanted a fake name, just in case this thing might cause future troubles. Everyone was okay with it. Then my uncle insisted that we get married in the hospital, which was very silly, but he knew how powerful my dad is and if he wanted, he could have brought lawyers to the hospital. This discussion took a very long time, but then we agreed we would marry in court and the Varmala ceremony would be at the hospital. It was March 1st, 2007.

*[Softly, looking at Ishan]* The next day, we all got dressed up and went to the court with the papers. Dad received a call from my aunt, saying that Shastri Uncle was insisting on signing as one of the witnesses. So, we had no choice but to go to the hospital. Sarthak, *aka* Raj, and I had to

sign, after which my Kaka and dad signed as witnesses. Thus, we were officially married.

Sarthak and I stayed with Kaka the whole day. Later, I asked Sarthak to leave, but he said he wanted to talk to me. So, we sat in the hospital corridor and talked the whole night. The next day, I had an award ceremony to attend. While I was coming back home that night, I received a call from my mom informing me that Kaka had passed away peacefully.

**Ishan:** *[Confused]* If that's the case, why did you tell us that you got married?

**Sash:** *[Softly, redirecting]* Oh, my Kaka happily called all the family members and, of course, asked me to tell you guys as he knew how important you all were to me. I even told him I would call you later, but he insisted. So, I called in front of him when I was in the hospital. I thought I would tell you all the exact reason later.

**Ishan:** *[Frustrated]* Why didn't you tell us then? What happened to Raj, I mean Sarthak? Why didn't you tell us the truth later?

**Sash:** *[Sighing, gathering courage]* So, when we got married, we spent the night together talking to each other outside Kaka's room in the hospital, and he was so handsome I couldn't take my eyes off him. He and I decided that we wanted to be in a relationship, and we would decide later if we wanted to get married to each other or not. Hence, we had asked my parents to never tell anyone that we weren't married.

## Back to March 3, 2007 *(10:20 am)*

**Sash:** *[Nervously, glancing at Sarthak]* Dad, can we talk to you for a moment?

**Dad**: *[Calmly]* Yes, tell me.

**Sash:** *[Taking a deep breath]* Could you please not tell anyone that we weren't married, in real? We started liking each other. I'm only 25, and I was not ready to get married, but we both think this is God's sign to keep us together. We really want to give this a try.

**Dad**: *[Sternly]* What nonsense!! God's sign? Because of your Kaka, you had to sign. But I've told my secretary to prepare divorce papers. I know a Judge. He's a very good friend of mine, so he will help us get through this process very fast before Sarthak joins my company, as I promised. *[Turning towards Sarthak]* And Sarthak, my secretary will call you between 12 pm to 1 pm to deliver the cheque I promised you.

**Sash:** *[Desperately]* Dad, it is God's sign. Don't you think so? How is it possible that when we were searching for a fake groom for me, we found him? Then how come Kaka forced us to get married in the hospital and we got married for real? How come we got attracted to each other in just one night? You know I had a lot of preferences in the man I wanted to marry, and Sarthak is a software engineer with no job right now, but why am I adoring him so much? Please, Dad, please let us be together.

**Sarthak**: *[Earnestly]* Sir, trust me, as long as I'm alive, I will never hurt your daughter, and I will never touch her without her permission.

**Dad:** *[Pausing, looking conflicted]* Give me some time to think.

**Sash:** *[Angrily]* Why do you need time to think, Dad? I've never asked you for anything ever. Why?

Sayesha was always a polite girl, but something happened to her that morning. Her facial features changed, and she started talking so loudly that the hospital staff had to request her to keep her voice down.

**Mom**: *[Firmly]* Sash, is this the way to talk to your father? We don't even know this man, and how can we allow you to be in a relationship with him?

**Sash:** *[Defiantly]* I'm not a child, Mom; I know what I'm doing.

**Sarthak**: *[Calmly]* What do you want to know about me, Ma'am?

**Sash:** *[Interrupting]* There's no need to tell anything about you, Sarthak. You have told me everything I need to know, and that's enough. Mom, Dad, I don't care at all. I like him, and I won't let anyone know that we married for a reason.

Sayesha's parents had never seen her like this before. She was so angry and frustrated. They argued for a long time, and when Sayesha didn't agree to their terms, they stepped away, thinking she was old enough to make her own decisions, and they agreed to the relationship.

**Sash:** *[Softly]* Thanks, Dad. Thank you, Mom.

**Sarthak**: Thank you, Sir and Ma'am. I promise, I won't ever hurt Sayesha.

**Mom**: Whatever. I don't care.

**Dad**: *[Disappointed]* We never wanted our firstborn to get married in such a way and to talk to us so rudely. We could have settled this after Uncle got out of the hospital, but she is behaving in a way I never expected.

**Sash:** Dad, I have never asked you for anything in my life. This is the first time I want something for myself. Please don't be angry. I am sorry.

**Dad**: *[Sighing]* You have never asked for anything because you got everything without even asking. Do you know how a dad feels to give away his daughter, especially to a strange man who he just met yesterday? Marriage is not a joke, but I don't expect you to understand that. Now, that you have married someone you just met.

**Sash:** Dad, please.

**Mom**: *[Resigned]* Leave it. Let her do whatever she wants. She will understand we were right after some time.

**Sash:** *[Hurt]* Mom, at least you understand.

**Mom**: *[Firmly]* I would have, my child, but the way you spoke to your father was intolerable. You should remember, for me he comes first, then both my daughters.

**Sash:** *[Desperately]* I don't know, Mom, but I have started liking him.

**Mom**: *[Softly]* Then date him; don't just put a married label on yourself.

**Sarthak**: *[Interjecting]* Uncle told everyone in the family. The label is already there, so don't you think it's better if we try to work this marriage out?

**Mom**: *[Irritated]*This is not a marriage, Son. It was a wedding. There is a huge difference between the two. A wedding is just a contract between two people, while marriage is a promise to be together forever. Marriage is pure and something to be loved and cherished. It is where not only you, but your souls unite, and it is not possible after just meeting once. Anyways, all the best to you both for your wedding.

**Dad**: *[Sarcastically]* Congratulations on your wedding.

**Sash:** *[Irritated]* Thanks, Dad. Sarthak, let's go from here, please. I can't listen to both of them. I don't know why they are unable to understand me.

**Sarthak**: *[Reassuringly]* It's okay, Sash. They will understand sooner or later. Hey, you have an award ceremony today, right?

**Sash:** *[Softly]* Yes, would you like to come with me?

**Sarthak**: *[Gently]* No, I have to go somewhere. I'll see you when you're back.

### July 25, 2009

**Sash:** *[Reflecting]* So, I was very happy that day, and then at night, as I told you, my Kaka passed away. We were busy with the rituals for a few days. I tried calling Sarthak, but his phone was not reachable. I was worried, but I didn't have anything to do except wait for him.

**Ishan:** After that, I remember your parents moved to Chicago by the end of March. When we met you at the airport that day, you said Raj was at a conference, so he couldn't come.

**Sash:** *[Nodding]* All of us planned to move to Chicago as it was becoming increasingly difficult for my dad to stay in that house without Kaka. He developed post-traumatic stress disorder. The doctor recommended that he relocate, and since Dad had already bought a house in Chicago years ago, we thought it would be great to move there. They all asked me to come too, but I insisted on finding Sarthak, so I stayed. My dad was furious with me because he couldn't understand why I suddenly became so infatuated with a random stranger. You know, Sarthak didn't even cash the cheque. Dad didn't talk to me for a while, but one day I missed him so much that I texted him saying I found Sarthak. I told him that Sarthak had met with an accident that day, so he wasn't responding. His phone got damaged. He called me the moment he was out of the hospital after he got his contacts back. He was happy to hear that, but he's still angry about why I left the whole family because of Sarthak. Since that day, he has never called me. I just talk to my sister and mom sometimes, but I have never told them what is going on in my life.

**Ishan:** *[Concerned]* Have they never asked you- "Where is Sarthak? Can we talk to him?"

**Sash:** *[Sighing]* They have but I end up giving new excuses all the time. Sometimes, I feel they know something is going on, but they never ask, and I never tell them anything.

It's strange how when we are young, our mom doesn't tell us things because we might get worried and when we get old, we don't tell her things for the same reason. Sometimes, I feel I just need my mom so that I can put my head on her lap and sleep. I know my mom would find a solution instantly, but I don't want to give her more stress.

**Ishan:** *[Gently]* You should have listened to your dad, Sash. I don't have parents, so I always wished I had someone to help me make decisions, but I had to do everything independently. You have parents; you are lucky, but you still do not understand. Don't feel bad, but that's the truth. People usually don't value what they have; instead, they chase after what they want.

How would your mom feel after seeing you like this? The little girl she gave birth to was confident and strong; the same girl now is so weak that she is taking pills to live.

**Sash:** *[Tearfully]* Yes, I know, and I regret it. If I tell my mother, she will break after seeing me like this, I know. That's the reason I have not told her anything. See, parents want to see their kids happy all the time but when it is not possible, we tend to lie to them so that they can live happily. Ishan, I want to meet my mother once, hug her and kiss her before I die.

**Ishan:** *[Firmly]* Shut up, Sash. You will be good in a few days and then you too move to Chicago. Your parents would be happy.

**Sash:** *[With a faint smile]* I just wish. Touchwood. Hey, Ishan, I completely forgot, it's almost 3 am. He will come soon. Please go back to your house.

**Ishan:** *[Confused]* Who will come?

**Sash:** *[Softly]* Raj.

**Ishan:** *[Alarmed]* Are you mad, Sash? Are you in a relationship with him? Are you guys married? Where is he now? He's not Raj, he's Sarthak, right? Tell me, please. I'm totally confused.

**Sash:** *[With a sigh]* I can't tell you anything more now. We will talk tomorrow. Please understand and go now.

**Ishan:** *[Stubbornly]* I'm not leaving you here alone. It seems scary. Either you come with me, or I'm staying the night.

**Sash:** *[Frustrated]* I can't come with you. Why don't you understand? Things are not that easy.

**Ishan:** Then, why don't you tell me what happened?

**Sash:** I will tell you, but not now.

**Ishan:** Then, when?

**Sash:** After I am done with the ritual.

**Ishan:** *[Baffled]* What ritual?

**Sash:** *[In a sharp tone]* You will find out soon. Okay, if you want to stay, I'll give you something to wear. Go change and sit quietly. If I do something, do not stop me.

**Ishan:** *[Worried]* What the hell are you talking about, Sash? You were not so secretive before.

**Sash:** *[Firmly]* Shh...Just wear this black kurta.

After a few minutes of argument, Ishan agreed to wear the kurta and sat in the corner as Sayesha asked him to. She switched off the lights and started lighting candles in her house. Then she brought out a whole chicken and placed it in the middle of the living room, marking a red circle around it with vermillion. She retrieved 3 knives from her room and placed them beside the chicken. She began muttering some mantras. The room started changing colours. Ishan tried not to panic. He couldn't believe what he was witnessing.

**Ishan:** *[Whispering, nervously]* Sash, what is this?

**Sash:** *[Continuing the ritual, barely audible]* Stay calm, Ishan. Trust me.

As the candles flickered and shadows danced on the walls, the atmosphere grew heavy. Ishan's heart pounded in his chest as he watched Sayesha perform the ritual. Her eyes were closed, and her chants grew louder, echoing in the room. The colors in the room seemed to pulse with each word she spoke.

The room had taken on an eerie, orange and blue hue, mimicking the morning light. The flames of the candles had turned green. Curtains fluttered as if caught in a gentle breeze, and a lamp in the corner had turned on by itself. Wind chimes rang melodiously, adding to the surreal atmosphere. Sayesha had a wide smile on her face, which unnerved Ishan. She was wearing a black saree with bridal jewellery, including a necklace, earrings, and bangles.

Vermilion adorned her forehead. Her hair was tied up neatly, and she sat straight in the northeast corner of the circle. When she finished the mantras, tears welled up in her eyes.

**Sash:** *[Softly, with a strange serenity]* Three new knives.

Suddenly, the chicken was crushed into bits. The knives hovered in the air, approaching Sayesha's wrist. Sayesha deliberately cut her skin, causing herself to bleed. Then, some blood was sucked into the air, leaving a mark on her hand. The room plunged into darkness as the candle flames extinguished. Sayesha stood up, switched on all the lights, and lay down on the couch.

**Ishan:** *[Horrified]* What the hell was that, Sash?

**Sash:** *[Weary]* Go sleep in the guest room. We'll talk tomorrow. I do this every day. I'm tired.

Afterward, she picked up the knives, hid them under her pillow, and went to bed without even changing. Ishan couldn't sleep the whole night. He knew something paranormal was happening in the house. He wanted to protect Sayesha. He started reflecting on the past, remembering how after Sayesha's fake marriage, she hadn't had time to call her friends, and they were all angry at her. Even when Ava had her first child, Sayesha didn't respond to the invitation for a Puja, claiming her phone was off. They had tried to meet Sayesha many times, but she had refused every time. They were so angry they decided never to speak to her again. Then, after two years, Sayesha called them all on a conference call on June 24th, 2009, inviting them to dinner at her house. Nobody wanted to go, but she begged and apologized, so they went. He realized that literally no one had spoken to Sayesha on the phone in the last two years since her marriage. They mostly texted her, and maybe if they had spoken, they would have known she wasn't well. He cursed himself and his friends for being so selfish. He remembered texting Sayesha on March 4th, 2007, and she replied, "I'm away. I'll see you all soon."

The next morning, Sayesha woke up at 8 a.m. Ishan was already awake, his eyes weary from a sleepless night.

**Ishan:** *[Concerned]* Are you okay, Sash?

**Sash:** *[Yawning]* I am fine. I am just tired. I don't feel like getting up, but I have work to do.

**Ishan:** *[Anxiously]* You promised me you would tell me everything in the morning. I couldn't sleep the whole night.

**Sash:** *[Puzzled]* What? Why?

**Ishan:** *[Frustrated]* Why? Because of the haunting rituals you did last night, because of what I saw last night. I am scared, Sash. Please don't ditch me. Please complete the whole story. Is there any Raj or not? Is he a ghost or a human? Who were you talking to last night? Please answer my questions.

**Sash:** *[Holding up a hand, her voice trembling slightly]* All right, all right, stop talking. I will tell you, but I need a nice coffee first.

**Ishan:** *[Nodding, eager to understand]* Okay, done.

He made her coffee, and they both sat on the balcony.

**Ishan:** *[Gently probing]* Could you now please finish yesterday's story and tell me what happened last night?

**Sash:** *[Taking a deep breath, her voice heavy with sorrow]* Okay, yes. So, after my Kaka passed away and all the rituals were complete, I tried calling Sarthak, but he didn't pick up. So, I waited for a month. Then, on April 9th, I went to the hospital to see if they could find his address. They checked, but they couldn't find anything related to his family. I was sad. Then, I met Dr. Samar on the way out. Do you remember him? He transferred to our school when we were in seventh standard.

**Ishan:** *[Frowning, trying to recall]* Yes, I know him.

**Sash:** *[Nodding, her voice tinged with nostalgia]* Yes, so he helped me find the address through hospital logs. He made a shocking revelation. He told me there was a patient named Sarthak Roy. He was admitted in the room next to my Kaka's room and passed away on March 1st, early morning around 2:30 am-3:00 a.m.

**Ishan:** *[Eyes widening in disbelief]* What the hell is going on?

**Sash:** *[Sighing deeply, her voice breaking]* I had the same question. But since I had the address, I decided to go and check it out. So, I went to his house, and some Raghu Kaka, his servant opened the door. I saw Sarthak's picture frame on a side table. When I met his mother, she confirmed Sarthak's death. I was alone and cried like hell. I couldn't believe I had married a dead man. I came back home. It wasn't easy for me to get over it. I fell into depression; I tried therapy and medications. I visited several temples hoping to find someone who could help me, but I found no one.

**Ishan:** *[Concerned, his voice soft]* Why didn't you call any of us?

**Sash:** *[Shaking her head, her eyes filled with pain]* I wasn't in the mental state to tell anyone. I didn't even tell my parents. They still don't know what's going on.

**Ishan:** *[Confused, searching for answers]* Then who were you talking to last night? What were you doing chanting all those mantras?

**Sash:** *[Holding up a hand to stop him, her voice weary]* Let me finish my story, Ishan. On June 6th, around 5 pm, I was alone in my bedroom when I heard a voice. I rushed out to the living room and saw Sarthak standing there.

**Ishan:** *[Eyes wide in disbelief]* Are you serious?

**Sash:** *[Nodding, her voice trembling]* I was shocked to see him. I ran to hug him, crying, telling him his mother lied about his death. But he didn't say a word. Two minutes later, I realized I was hugging thin air. I thought I was losing my mind until I found a note in the kitchen:

"My mother was right." Since then, whenever I have doubts, I get these notes from him.

**Ishan:** *[Connecting the dots, realization dawning]* And he told you earlier, "I am all alone now", at the garden which meant he is alone wherever he is and not that his family died. He died and is now alone, probably in need of a partner.

**Sash:** *[Nodding slowly, her voice breaking]* Probably. He comes every day around 3:10 am, trying to ask me for some help. I consulted a tantric who gave me mantras to keep him away. I don't know how much longer I can handle this. It's been a year and a half, Ishan. I had almost forgotten my previous life until I saw Ava with her son in the garden and thought of calling you all.

**Ishan:** *[Confused and concerned]* Ava never mentioned any of this.

**Sash:** *[Softly, almost whispering]* Because she didn't know I was watching.

**Ishan:** *[Puzzled]* Wait, tell me one more thing. If there is no Raj, who called you last night?

**Sash:** *[Sighing, her voice heavy with exhaustion]* I called myself purposely. I had my phone with me in one hand. When I saw you came back, I knew you would ask when Raj is going to come back home so I did all of this to make you realize that he is busy and will be back by morning. I was not planning to tell you the complete story.

**Ishan:** *[Understanding, but still worried]* Oh ok, I can understand. Why did you cut yourself at night with a knife if Sarthak does not want to hurt you?

**Sash:** *[Frustration and despair evident in her voice]* I am done with all these things. I have tried to kill myself, multiple times as I don't know what he wants. He always comes back with a question—Knife? I have literally got more than 300 knives and I have no idea what kind of knife he is talking about. So, I got frustrated and once tried to kill myself during the ritual, but you know what happened? The blood vanished and my cut healed leaving a mark. Sometimes, I feel he wants me to be with him but then he does not allow me to kill myself, I am all confused.

**Ishan:** *[Shocked, voice full of concern]* Oh my God. Tell me, Sash, how can I help you now?

**Sash:** *[Desperation in her voice]* I have no idea. I feel crushed. Sometimes I think ending my life might be the only way to make him leave me alone.

**Ishan:** *[Firmly, trying to calm her]* Are you crazy? You're never doing that. Promise me.

**Sash:** *[Weakly, but sincerely]* Okay, I promise, but I can't live like this forever.

**Ishan:** *[Determined]* We'll find a solution. Let me call everyone and tell them everything. We need their help.

**Sash:** *[Shaking her head, her voice firm]* No, I can't involve anyone else in this mess. It's just you and me now, forever.

**Ishan:** *[Worried but accepting]* You're scaring me. Okay, fine. Can we try talking to Sarthak's spirit or whatever it is and ask if there's anything else we can do to make him leave you alone?

**Sash:** *[Tiredly, almost dismissively]* This isn't a movie.

**Ishan:** *[Persistently]* I know, but there has to be something. Maybe we can see a priest or someone.

**Sash:** *[Sighing deeply, her voice exhausted]* I'm exhausted, Ishan. I think I would take a nap now.

**Ishan:** *[Gently, trying to be practical]* We haven't eaten since morning. It's already 12:30 pm. Should I make something to eat or order something?

**Sash:** *[Softly, her energy waning]* No, I'll sleep. You go home and rest. We'll meet in the evening.

## Chapter - 3
# ISHAN'S DARK DISCOVERY

Reluctant to leave Sayesha alone, Ishan decided to stay and rest in the guest bedroom. Unable to sleep, he went to Sayesha's room when she was deeply asleep. He found the notes he had seen in her room yesterday and brought them to the living room. After hours of pondering, he finally cracked the code. Rushing back to Sayesha's room, he started waking her up. She snapped, "What do you want, Ishan?"

**Ishan:** *[Urgently]* I cracked the code.

**Sash:** *[Confused and groggy]* What code?

**Ishan:** *[Determined]* I know you kept the knives under your pillow because Sarthak asked you to.

**Sash:** Yeah, so?

**Ishan:** *[Excitedly]* Sash, he doesn't want a knife. He wants K.N.I.F.E.

**Sash:** Either you've lost it, or I'm dreaming.

**Ishan:** *[Insistent]* Sash, what he wrote wasn't about the knife we use in the kitchen. It's a code. It means something. He put a dot after every letter. He keeps coming here, asking you if you found K.N.I.F.E., but you're thinking of it differently.

**Sash:** *[Frustrated]* Ishan, I have like 300-350 knives in my house. I thought he wanted a knife.

**Ishan:** No, Sash, there's something else. Think about him. How did he look? How did he talk? Did he ever mention anything unusual?

Sayesha's mind raced as she recalled Sarthak saying, "When we officially marry, I'll give you the necklace, my grandfather gave me. I want to give it to you now, but he made me promise to keep it in the family estate." She had declined, saying she only sought true love. But he insisted it wasn't an ordinary necklace; his grandfather claimed it could make dreams come true—make someone famous and wealthy.

She laughed it off, but Sarthak was serious. "I can prove it," he said. "Many people are after that necklace, but I've hidden it in a secret safehouse."

**Ishan:** That's it.

It was late evening, and Sayesha decided to order food.

**Sash:** Do you want anything to eat?

**Ishan:** Just get me an egg roll.

**Sash:** Okay.

After 50 minutes, the doorbell rang. It was the delivery boy.

**Delivery Boy:** *[Promptly]* "Ma'am, the ice cream might melt, so please keep it in the fridge early or it'll spoil."

**Sash:** Yes, sure.

**Ishan:** *[Curious]* What did he say?

**Sash:** Nothing. You said you wanted an egg roll, so I ordered that for you, plus a cheeseburger and Chocofudge ice cream for both of us. I've been craving sweets lately. And I know you love ice cream, so I got one for you.

**Ishan:** *[Persistent]* No, Sash, I mean what did the delivery guy say?

**Sash:** *[Reiterating]* Ma'am, the ice cream might melt, so please keep it in the fridge early or it'll spoil.

**Ishan:** *[Realizing]* Keep it in Fridge Early... Keep it in Fridge Early... Keep it in Fridge Early...

**Sash:** What are you saying?

Ishan *[Pulling Sash towards the dining table and scribbling]* See this...

**Ishan:** *[Showing the code]*

**K** - Keep,

**N** - Necklace,

**I** - In,

**F** - Family,

**E** - Estate.

"Keep the necklace in our family estate." That's what Sarthak meant.

**Sash:** *[Dumbfounded, feeling a mix of relief and frustration]* I can't believe I missed this.

**Sash:** What should we do then? Should we try to find the necklace? But even if we find it, Sarthak is gone. Who would we give it to?

**Ishan:** His family, of course.

**Sash:** *[Worried]* What if they accuse us of stealing it?

**Ishan:** Sash, that doesn't make sense. If we stole it, why would we return it?

**Sash:** Okay, so what's our next step? Should we go to his house again?

**Ishan:** No, first we need to confirm with Sarthak if he was referring to the necklace. We need to 'CALL' him.

**Sash:** He might come tonight.

**Ishan:** *[Insistent]* 'Might' won't cut it this time. We have to wrap this up quickly so you can get better.

**Sash:** *[Hesitant]* I know a psychic who can help, but he won't do it for free.

**Ishan:** *[Curious]* How much money are we talking about?

**Sash:** No, he doesn't want money. He'll want to borrow your soul for a while to finish someone else's unfinished business.

**Ishan:** *[Shocked]* What? Soul? How? And why would we do someone else's job?

**Sash:** So, basically...

**Ishan:** Hold on, hold on. Sash, we need the whole gang involved. Let me tell everyone so they can help us find the necklace.

**Sash:** *[Pleading]* No, Ishan, I cannot involve everyone else, like I told you earlier. Please understand.

After much contemplation, Sayesha finally agreed to call everyone. *[Ishan contacted Ava, asking her to gather everyone at Sayesha's house. It was already 10:15 pm, and Ava was worried that something had gone wrong.]*

**Ishan:** *[Urgently]* Hi Ava, I need you and the gang to come to Sash's house immediately.

**Ava:** *[Concerned]* Why? What happened? Is everything alright?

**Ishan:** A lot of things have happened. Please come soon, and yes, do you remember the party we had at your lake house, the day Sash got married suddenly?

**Ava:** Yes, I do.

**Ishan:** We met Sarthak there, right?

**Ava:** *[Confused]* Who's Sarthak?

**Ishan:** Sorry, not Sarthak. Raj. We met Raj, right?

**Ava:** Yes, Sash and Raj both were there. We danced the whole night and celebrated their wedding.

**Ishan:** Do you remember how he looked?

**Ava:** Yes, a little. We were drunk, and then I only met him once, so I don't remember that much. But yes, we clicked pictures.

**Ishan:** Yes, I want those pictures.

**Ava:** Ok, I will get the whole gang and the pictures of my party are on my phone.

**Ishan:** Great, come soon.

She quickly rallied the group, and by the time they arrived at Sayesha's place, Ishan and Sayesha had finished dinner. It was 11:30 pm.

## Chapter - 4
## THE HIDDEN FEAR

**Ding Dong...**

**Sash:** *[Lightly exasperated]* Can you put the plates in the kitchen? I'll get the door.

**Ishan:** Sure, okay.

Sayesha opened the door, Ava and Nisha enveloped her in a group hug.

**Sash:** *[Struggling to breathe]* Guys, stop. I can't breathe. What's going on?

**Nisha:** *[Concerned]* Ava said something happened to you, so we all got worried.

**Sash:** To me?

**Ava:** No, Ishan called and said something happened. I thought...

**Sash:** *[Frustrated]* Yeah, so you thought something happened to me. Great!

**Kush:** Obviously.

**Ava:** *[Demanding]* Okay, now tell us what's going on.

**Sash:** *[Deferring]* Ishan will explain.

**Ishan:** *[Seriously]* When we came here yesterday, I found knives, notes, and confessions in Sash's room.

**Kush:** What??? Are you serious? Why didn't you tell us yesterday.

**Ishan:** *[Calmly]* How can I tell you about her personal stuff without asking her? Let me finish, and then you can react.

Ishan proceeded to recount the entire story to the rest of the group. They were shocked, surprised, and scared—hard to believe they were discussing the same Sayesha they had seen just a day earlier, envying her seemingly perfect life. Ava hugged Sayesha and cried deeply, feeling remorseful for her earlier comments about Sayesha's luck.

**Ava:** *[Apologetic, tearful]* I'm sorry, Sash. I didn't realize how difficult things were for you.

**Sash:** *[Gently]* It's okay, Ava. But now we need a plan to find that necklace.

**Ishan:** I have a simple idea. Let's go to Sarthak's house, talk to his mother, and ask about the necklace. We'll explain everything. She can find it and keep it in a safe place.

**Sash:** *[Skeptical]* Hmm, that sounds too easy. If that were the case, Sarthak would be haunting his mother, not me.

**Kush:** *[Laughing]* Haha, good point.

**Ava:** It's not funny, Kush. We need to do something.

**Kush:** I get it, but are we sure he was talking about a necklace? What if we misinterpreted the code?

**Ishan:** *[Thoughtful]* That's a valid concern. Sash and I discussed it, and she knows a tantric or someone who might be able to help, but it involves trading souls or something.

**Kush:** *[Disbelieving]* Are you serious? My soul?

**Sash:** *[Nodding]* Yes.

**Nisha:** How?

**Sash:** *[Explaining in a soft tone]* Well, if you want help, you have to help someone else who's searching for answers. For example: If I need help, I will not do astral travel for my purpose; someone else will. If they need help, I will have to trade my soul, helping them find their answers. There's one more thing—you can't go twice, and only one person can go at a time.

They have to complete the task, or they could die.

**Ishan:** *[Confused]* I'm lost here. We help, and we might die? Why can't we just wait for Sarthak tonight?

**Kush:** *[Curious]* Astral travel? Is it a real thing?

**Sash:** Yes, Kush, it is. I have seen that horrifying thing myself.

**Nisha:** Or better yet, why don't we find the necklace ourselves and verify if it's the right thing?

**Sash:** Actually, we need to do that quickly. We only have a month left.

**Ishan:** *[Pressing]* What else aren't you telling us?

**Sash:** *[Regretful, serious]* When I saw Sarthak in June 2007, I knew something was wrong. The first thing I did was go to the Tantric. He helped me connect with Sarthak, who only conveyed that he needed 'knife'. I was clueless. The Tantric warned me: I had six months to fulfil his request, or he might take over my body to complete the task himself. If that happens, I might not survive, and it could unleash chaos upon our world. When I asked how certain he was, the Tantric said it usually ends that way. Finding a simple knife proved elusive, and after six months of trying, I heard a scream in my living room. Sarthak had returned, but not to harm me. He wept bitterly, revealing he didn't wish to do this. His father and grandfather's soul were ensnared by an evil force, demanding the very knife Sarthak alone could retrieve. If he succeeds, his family's souls find peace; if not, they face torment indefinitely.

**Kush:** *[Inquisitive, skeptical]* So, you went to this Tantric, potentially traded your soul—am I right? How did he communicate with Sarthak? Spirits talking? Sounds like something out of a movie. Why you? And how did you even find this Tantric? Also, this one-month deadline—is that real?

**Sash:** *[Hesitant, wary]* I can't disclose everything.

**Nisha:** *[Firmly]* Sash, for us to help, we need the truth.

**Sash:** *[Pleading]* Promise me you won't judge or back out. You can leave now, but not after I tell you everything.

**Ava:** *[Anxious, protective]* Sash, this is scary. I have a daughter to think about. If I die, what happens to her? And Nisha's situation... her life is complicated. I'm sorry, but I can't get involved.

**Ishan:** *[Appealing]* Remember all the times Sash was there for us?

**Kush:** *[Determined]* I'm in. Sash needs us.

**Nisha:** *[Resolutely]* Me too.

**Ishan:** *[Supportive]* Me too.

**Ava:** *[Regretful]* I'll have to opt out. I'm sorry. *[Leaves quickly.]*

**Sayesha:** *[Touched]* Thank you all for your support.

**Nisha:** *[Locking the door]* For privacy.

**Kush:** *[Making an effort to ease the tension]* I'll make coffee for everyone.

After 10 minutes, they heard the doorbell. Nisha opened the door, only to find Ava standing outside.

**Nisha:** What happened? Did you forget something?

**Ava:** *[Smiling with a hint of sarcasm]* No, I was thinking about what I would do alone if you all died. So, I'm in. Let's solve this mystery together.

**Sash:** *[Grateful]* You really don't have to do this, Ava.

**Ava:** *[Decisive]* I know, Sash. I thought it over downstairs in the parking lot. I called Raunak and told him I'm staying over. Sash needs me. We'll figure this out together. Besides, you know I'm great at solving mysteries.

**Sash:** *[Concerned]* But what about your daughter?

**Ava:** *[Light-hearted]* Oh, she will survive with another 'sexy mom', if anything happens to me. Haha.

**Ishan:** Don't worry, we will not let anything happen to you.

**Kush:** *[Handing out coffee]* Here, have some coffee. It might help.

**Ishan:** *[Serious]* Alright, Sash. Can you answer all the questions Kush asked earlier?

**Sash:** *[Nervous]* You promised not to judge.

**Ava:** *[Reassuring]* We won't, Sash.

**Sash:** *[Taking a deep breath, starting her story]* I didn't go to a Tantric right away when I realized Sarthak was back. I went to the nearby Hanuman temple. There, I met a lady distributing sweets. She saw I was upset and asked what was wrong. Scared and sweating, I confessed I had unknowingly married a spirit. She understood and mentioned knowing about spirits returning to finish unfinished business. She took me to the Tantric who explained I'd have to offer my soul for any communication. Reluctant, I sought someone willing, and the building janitor volunteered, unaware of the risk that he could die too. I went to the Tantric who asked a man to help me as it was not allowed for me or the janitor to go there. I had already told you the reason. As discussed earlier after this man would help us, janitor would be the next to help someone else. During the ritual, that man entered a trance, described seeing three men—one young man crying and asking for a 'knife', a middle-aged man and one older man tied with chains. After that, it was the janitor's turn.

**Kush:** *[Worried]* Please tell me he didn't die.

**Sash:** *[Tearfully]* He didn't make it. I can't live with this guilt. I never meant for any of this to happen.

**Ishan:** *[Angry, gripping Sayesha's arms]* Do you realize, Sash, you caused someone's death?

**Sash:** *[Breaking down]* I'm so sorry, guys.

**Ishan:** *[Resolute, upset]* Once this is over, we're handing you over to the police.

**Sash:** Please don't. My life is already a nightmare. Why are you doing this?

**Nisha:** *[Shouting]*Because it's right, Sash. You need help.

**Kush:** Tell us more. What happened next?

**Sash:** I didn't find answers, so I turned to social media and finally found a psychic who communicates with the dead.

**Ishan:** *[Fuming]* Unbelievable.

**Sash:** I went to her. She had her own rituals where she goes into a trance. She had a pen and paper with her. She started writing very fast, faster than I could have ever imagined. Then she looked at me and asked, "He needs help with his unfinished work." I immediately agreed to help him with anything, and since then, he has been haunting me. He hasn't tried to harm me physically, but I feel like time is running out to complete his task before that evil spirit might kill me. After she finished all the rituals, we read what she wrote, and it described everything I've told you earlier.

**Kush:** *[Sarcastically impressed]* So, you brought this problem upon yourself. Wow, I'm impressed, Sash. What were you thinking?

**Sash:** *[Emotionally]* I was in love with Sarthak.

**Ava:** *[Disbelieving, angry]* Seriously? You met him once, had a fake marriage with him, and now you claim to be in love? This is beyond belief. You've studied so much that you've lost your mind.

**Sash:** *[Defensively]* It was not a fake marriage.

**Ava:** *[Angrily]* Yeah, right. One day marriage is real.

**Kush:** *[Inquisitive]* Why do you think you have a month left?

**Sash:** *[Uneasily]* I don't know, but I had a dream a few days ago. There was this incredibly ugly man who told me I only have a month to live. He warned me to finish the task quickly.

**Kush:** *[Doubtful]* So, you think that's reality? It could have just been a weird dream, Sash.

**Ava:** So, summarizing the whole story: Your uncle forced you into a marriage, which turned out to be with a spirit who disappeared later. You found a lady at the temple who took you to a tantric. You ended up inadvertently causing the death of an old man. Then you found a psychic who told you what the spirit wants. Sarthak's grandfather and father are also dead and caught by an evil spirit who wants K.N.I.F.E. We're not even sure if we've cracked the right code. Now, you want us to go to the tantric and potentially trade our souls to confirm if the code is correct, all while your husband might or might not show up tonight to validate our findings. And you believe we have only one month left.

**Sash:** *[Nodding]* Yes, that's the truth.

**Ishan:** *[Concerned]* Have you hidden anything else from us?

**Sash:** *[Pleading]* No, Ishan. Please don't be angry with me.

**Ishan:** *[Softening, still troubled]* I'm not angry. I'm just disturbed that I'm helping someone involved in a death, and I feel sorry for you. What have you gotten yourself into? This isn't good. Guys, whatever we decide to do now is very dangerous. Fighting a SPIRIT isn't easy.

**Sash:** *[Apologetic]* I'm sorry for dragging you all into this.

**Nisha:** *[Harshly]* Oh, you should be, Sash.

**Kush:** *[Resolutely]* It's okay, but what do we do now?

**Ishan:** *[Decisive]* I think we should go to the tantric, and I'll be the one to trade my soul.

**Kush:** *[Questioning]* Why you?

**Sash:** *[Firmly]* No, this time I'll do it.

**Ishan:** *[Loudly]* Just shut up, Sash. You all have families, and I want Sash to end up in jail. She should reap what she has sown. If she goes for astral travel, she might die, and that would be easier than going to jail. So, I will go. I'm alone. I'm an orphan. No one will miss me. Make sure to turn her in to the police if something happens to me.

**Kush:** *[Speaking softly]* Relax, Ishan. If we decide to do this, we need to think calmly. And if something happens, we will miss you. Don't you dare say you don't have family. We are your family.

**Ishan:** *[Angrily]* Please, Kush, this is not the time to get emotional. So, early morning, tomorrow, we'll go to the Tantric. It's already 2 AM.

**Sash:** *[Determined]* Actually, we could go now. If we leave now, we'll reach there by 3:30 AM, and according to the Tantric, 4 AM is the best time for astral travel.

**Nisha:** *[Sarcastically]* Wow, you've done a PhD on spirits and astral travel, haven't you?

**Sash:** *[Emotional]* Please don't mock me. I've already been through a lot.

**Ishan:** *[Bitterly]* Yes, we know. The person who kills someone goes through a lot.

**Kush:** Ishan, be quiet.

**Ishan:** Okay, let's go then.

**Ava:** *[Curious]* Ishan, why did you ask for my party's pictures?

**Ishan:** *[Apologetic]* Oh, yes. I completely forgot. Show me those pictures.

**Ava:** *[Handing over her phone]* See, here they are. We were drunk and there was all fog near the lake, so the pictures are a little blurred.

**Ishan:** *[Examining the photo]* It's alright. Let me see. Sash, can you see this picture? You and Raj are right here in this photo.

**Sash:** *[Shocked]* Show me... How did this happen? I swear I was with my uncle that night. I cannot believe this. How come we are celebrating with you all.

**Nisha:** *[Gently]* Sash, please don't get hurt, but is it possible that whatever you are doing or thinking is just in your mind and not reality?

**Sash:** *[Defensive]* What are you saying? Am I delusional?

**Nisha:** *[Calmly]* See, I am just asking you. Just think about it, as we were all there at the party. It's not like just Ishan or Ava saw you both. I and Kush were there too. We met you guys.

**Sash:** *[Frustrated]* Do you know, Nisha, what I am going through? I have seen a psychiatrist as well. I am taking my medications, but nothing is helping. Please, for once, trust me for what I am saying. Please. Let's go.

**Kush:** *[Pragmatically]* I think the best way to find out if Sash is delusional or not is to go to that Tantric's place. If he recognizes her, it will mean she is telling us the truth, or else she is lying.

**Ishan:** *[Resolutely]* Okay, but Sash, if you are lying this time, do not consider me your friend going forward.

**Ava:** *[Reasoning]* One second. If she is lying or she is delusional, it will mean she has not murdered anyone, which is the good news.

**Kush:** *[Supportively]* Yes. So, let's go then.

**Ava:** I'll drive. Sash, lock the house. Nisha, call the elevator.

**Nisha:** Okay.

**Sash:** *[Gathering items]* Let me grab the notes.

**Nisha:** *[Curious]* What notes?

**Sash:** The ones Ishan mentioned—threat notes.

**Nisha:** Ahh…Okay

## Chapter - 5
## THE FORBIDDEN RITUAL

Sayesha picked up the notes and locked the door. They headed to the parking lot where Ava had the car ready. Everyone got in, and Sayesha directed Ava to the Tantric's place. The car ride was silent. The weather was pleasant, with a cool wind blowing through the windows. Everyone was curious about their destination. Sayesha guided them onto a quiet road that led past a house that looked haunted. Tall trees lined both sides of the road, swaying in the breeze under a dark sky. Abandoned buildings loomed across from them, old and dilapidated with broken windows and black tar stains on their white exteriors. Some doors creaked open as the wind passed through. The buildings seemed to have only white-painted bricks with no plaster. The numbers "563," "564," "566" were faintly painted in black on the buildings. There wasn't a single living being in sight, not even animals. They took a right turn near a large Banyan tree, arriving at a small house with a porch. This house also appeared old, with cracked walls, faded paint, and no lights around it.

**Sash:** *[Decisively]* Stop the car. We're here.

**Ava:** *[Nodding]* Okay.

They all got out of the car. Kush approached the house, passing through a small open gate. He reached the door where a small skull-shaped ornament hung. He knocked on it, and silence filled the air, interrupted only by the whistle of the wind. Instead of tiles, asymmetrical stones paved the ground. When no one answered, Kush knocked again.

An elderly woman opened the door and recognized Sayesha.

**Old Lady:** *[Harshly]* What do you want now? Planning to kill someone else?

**Sash:** *[Desperately]* Amma, I need to meet Kailash Baba.

**Old Lady:** *[Dismissively]* He's meditating. Leave now.

The lady turned towards her friends.

**Old Lady:** *[Accusingly]* Did she tell you she killed a man without his consent?

**Kush:** *[Inquiring]* Where's his body, Amma?

**Old Lady:** *[Indifferently]* It's near the lake. Can't you see it? It was useless. But his soul lingers near that lake. We keep his body preserved, just in case.

**Ava:** *[Confused]* What lake? Why preserve it?

**Old Lady:** *[Scornfully]* You don't have eyes ? Look left. There used to be a lake. She cursed our land. There's no water now. We need bodies for rituals sometimes. You're young, you won't understand.

**Sash:** *[Pleading]* Please, Amma, it's urgent. We must see Baba. The old lady stared at her for a moment before saying.

**Old Lady:** Wait here, I'll speak with him.

Ishan stood silently, contemplating his fate. Questions raced through his mind: "Will I also die?" "Why did I ask Sash what happened?" "Why did the universe choose me for this?" "Should I tell her I quit?" "No, I cannot do that either. I cannot ditch her like this."

**Old Lady:** *[Cautiously]* Come in, but quietly. Take your shoes off outside. I don't know whose souls they've brought with them.

Inside, the room was dimly lit with burning candles, a red book, and a red item hung on the wall. A small divan held Baba, sitting cross-legged across a table adorned with Rudraksha beads, stones, a large book, cards, and more candles. The old lady brought out chairs, indicating there were only two rooms in the house. They all sat facing Baba.

**Baba:** What do you want?

Baba spoke with a serious tone. His complexion was dark, with long tangled hair, big eyes, dark lips, yet a certain glow on his face. A scar ran across his left cheek as if burned, and he wore Tripundra on his forehead. Dressed in a red kurta and pyjama, he had multiple Rudraksha necklaces, large round wooden earrings, and rings on his fingers. The scent of incense hung around him, as if he hadn't bathed in a while.

**Ishan:** *[Determined]* Baba Ji, Sayesha told us everything. We want to help her. We think the spirit wasn't referring to a knife but a code. We need to speak with the spirit to confirm if we're right, or it'll continue haunting Sayesha.

**Baba:** *[Grimly]* You want to help her. You understand what that means, right? You're all accomplices in her crime. Her fate is sealed. She will die a painful death at the hands of Hari.

**Kush:** *[Confused]* Who is Hari?

**Sash:** *[Resigned]* The janitor. It's okay, Baba. I just want Sarthak to get what he wants. I don't care if I die after that.

**Ishan:** Is there any other way Sayesha can make up for her karma?

**Baba:** *[Solemnly]* Those are very difficult. Is she here to repent, or do you want to speak with Sarthak?

**Sash:** Both.

**Baba:** Who among you is ready for astral travel?

**Sash:** Can we talk directly to Sarthak? Last time, you sent someone else for us and had us do another person's work.

**Baba:** *[Patiently]* We help each other with our problems because it's hard to see a loved one suffering in another realm. This isn't a simple matter. When you journey for someone else, it's easier because your motivation is selfless. However, last time you made a mistake by bringing an elderly man without warning him of the dangers, solely for your selfish reasons. This time, your journey will be very challenging. You must travel alone, choose your own path, and later make amends for your sins. If you're ready, we can start the procedure in exactly five minutes. Take your time to think it over. Your friends can support you, but you must undertake the journey alone.

**Ishan:** *[Desperately]* Can I go with her?

**Baba:** Are you both married?

**Ishan:** *[Confused]* No, she's, my friend.

**Baba:** *[Firmly]* Souls connect if you're married. So, you cannot go.

**Ishan:** *[Pleading]* Is there any other way, please? I can't let her go alone. She's vulnerable.

**Baba:** *[Dismissive]* Do you love her?

**Ishan:** *[Defensively]* No, why?

**Baba:** Then why are you doing this for her?

**Ishan:** *[Emotionally]* I'm an orphan. She helped me when no one else did. I want to be there for her.

**Baba:** This is nonsense.

**Kush:** *[Supportively]* Please, Baba Ji. Let them go together.

**Baba:** *[Reluctantly]* Even if I send both of you, it won't be easy as there are places you must go alone. But I can do one thing. There's a forbidden ritual so you will have to suffer consequences. You both need to give some of your blood. If the spirits allow, then you can go together.

**Sash:** *[Resolutely]* It's okay, Ishan. I can do this alone.

**Ishan:** *[Firmly]* You've done enough alone. I don't trust you anymore. I must go with you, or you will attract some other problems. Baba, please start the ritual.

**Baba:** *[Nodding]* I will start the ritual now since it's already 4 am, and you need to be there before 4:30 am, here. Time moves differently in another realm. You must reach before it's 3:10 am there. The doors open sharp at 3:10 am.

**Nisha:** *[Anxiously]* What time is it there now?

**Baba:** *[Uncertainly]* I don't know. I've never travelled. I just know if you don't arrive before 3:10 am, you'll have to wait another day, which could lead to horrifying events. You might even die. We won't be able to bring you back unless your purpose is fulfilled.

Baba then started the ritual. He brought a copper bowl and placed inside two pairs of cloves, two hair-like threads, two cinnamon sticks, two wax squares, and eucalyptus oil. The smell was strong. Next, he took Sayesha and Ishan's hands and made a cut on their palms, causing blood to flow. He mixed their blood together in the bowl and gave them a neon-green cloth to tie. He lit it and said, "If the yellow flame turns green, it's a sign from the spirits that both of you can go together. If not, no one can go."

**Sash:** *[Panicked]* No one? I can't go alone.

**Baba:** *[Decisively]* No, now that you have a cut on your hand, you can't go alone because only a person without physical injuries can travel.

**Sash:** *[Frustrated]* Why didn't you tell us this before?

**Baba:** *[Coldly]* Quiet.

Baba then began chanting some strange mantras, and suddenly, everyone saw the flame turn green. They were relieved they could go together but also scared.

**Baba:** *[Seriously]* Both of you can go now. Remember this before I send you into a trance— FOLLOW THE SOUND and your wounds are your key to this universe. You have only 45 minutes before you must return, or you'll be stuck there for another 24 hours. If you do not come by then as well, you will be stuck forever like Hari.

Sash and Ishan said together, "Yes."

Baba seated them together on a chair, holding their hands. He told the others that while Sayesha and Ishan were in another universe, they might sense something unusual, but they shouldn't move or leave the house, no matter what happens.

**Baba:** *[Solemnly]* Stay where you are and don't leave the house, no matter what you sense. A strong spirit may come to guide them.

The others nodded in agreement, though unease was visible on their faces. Baba applied vermilion to Sayesha and Ishan's foreheads, then handed each of them a blue crystal.

**Baba:** *[Calmly]* Close your eyes and focus on the crystals as I chant.

As he began chanting mantras, the room seemed to brighten, revealing more details of Baba's house to the rest of the group. Skulls adorned the corners, casting eerie shadows.

Nisha caught sight of a shadow and felt panic rising within her.

**Ava:** *[Whispering]* It's okay, Nisha. Hold my hand.

The colours in the room took on a familiar hue, reminiscent of what Ishan had witnessed at Sayesha's house the previous night. A small open tin box sat before Sayesha and Ishan, filled with mysterious ingredients. Without warning, it ignited on its own, flames flickering to life. As Baba ceased his chanting, a solemn silence enveloped the room.

**Baba:** *[Authoritatively]* You both must return before this flame extinguishes.

Both Sayesha and Ishan nodded in solemn acknowledgment as Baba resumed his chanting of mantras.

After some time, a strange sensation gripped Sayesha and Ishan, pulling them as if into the depths of the earth. In the blink of an eye, they found themselves transported to another place. It felt as though they had been hurled into a dense jungle.

## Chapter - 6
# THE HAUNTED CONFRONTATION

Both looked at each other. They noticed the forest—a dense, dark expanse with ants crawling across the floor. Dead crows littered the ground, and towering trees seemed to connect heaven to earth.

They turned around to see what else was there and spotted a beautiful lake nearby. As they approached the lake, they noticed the area was arranged in the shape of a triangle, with trees planted so closely together they formed a boundary wall, effectively preventing any escape.

Standing near the lake, Ishan peered into the water and was horrified to see the bodies of water animals and human beings. The lake, initially appearing blue from a distance, was actually a red river—a river of blood.

**Ishan:** *[Fearfully]* It's... it's blood.

**Sayesha**: *[Holding his hand]* We must be in Pataal Lok... if such a place exists.

They moved away from the blood-red river and saw three men sitting and whispering among themselves. One had no leg, another's lips were torn, and the third wore a crooked smile. The only sources of light were fireflies, their countless numbers forming a glowing ceiling above them.

The fireflies seemed to be floating just out of reach, their proximity an illusion meant to trap souls.

There was no wind, making it increasingly difficult to breathe.

Ishan suddenly heard a rhythmic sound—tong, tong, tong...

**Ishan:** *[Determined]* Baba said to follow the sound. I think it's coming from that direction. They moved towards the right, the sound growing louder with each step they took.

Tong, tong, tong…

Tong, tong, tong …

Tong, tong, tong…

Tong, tong, tong…

Tong, tong, tong…

Tong, tong, tong…

Tong, tong, tong…

Tong, tong, tong…..

Tong, tong, tong…..

Tong, tong, tong…..

Tong, tong, tong….

Tong, tong, tong……

Sayesha felt a hand on her shoulder. She turned and saw something shocking.

**Sash:** *[Surprised and anxious]* Hari???

**Hari:** *[Desperate]* Are you here to take me? Take me away.

**Sash:** *[Determined]* No, I'm here to talk to Sarthak. Ishan?? Ishan???

It became so dark that she couldn't see Ishan or hear him. They held hands, but when the sound grew louder, they pulled apart to cover their ears. Sayesha was shocked; how could she hear Hari clearly but not Ishan? She tried to move away but found her leg stuck to the ground. Looking down, she saw Hari, holding her right leg and begging to be taken away— he had been trapped there for nearly two years.

**Sash:** *[Pleading and tearful]* Hari, let go, please. Are you alive?

**Hari:** *[Desperate]* I haven't gone to heaven or hell. My soul is trapped. I've tried to come back, but the doors to the other world closed. Only a living soul can take me back. My body is near the lake, not yet burned. Please, take me with you.

**Sash:** *[Crying]* Please, help me find Ishan. Ishan?? Ishan?? Hari, I promise I'll take you back, but help me find Ishan.

**Hari:** *[in a ghostly voice]* You're standing on the crow, and the oath you just made binds you. Whatever you promise here, you must fulfil, or the consequences will be dangerous.

She looked down and saw she was standing on a dead crow. She jumped, hands in the air, and Ishan noticed the neon cloth on her hand. He held her hand, pulled her closer, and hugged her.

**Sash:** *[Screaming]* AHHHHHHHHH....

**Ishan:** *[Comforting]* Shh. shh. I'm here.

**Sash:** *[Panicked]* I can't hear you, Ishan. I found Hari, and we have to take him with us.

**Ishan:** *[Shouting]* I cannot hear you.

Ishan moved further right and found a huge clock. It looked like the moon on earth, with numbers etched into it like a clock face. It was enormous, glistening white with dust obscuring the numbers. The hands moved, making the "TONG" noise. Ishan checked the time; it was 3:09 am. He remembered Baba's words: the doors open at 3:10 am. They waited a minute, and exactly at 3:10 am, a strong wind blew, trees swayed, and all the dead animals were drawn into the clock, which turned dark red, as if a fire burned inside.

Ishan grabbed Sayesha's hand and jumped into the clock. Inside, everything was red: red barren land, red mountains, red trees, red clouds, and red houses. People, animals, and birds moved slowly, as if in another world without sound. It was eerily silent, and time seemed to have slowed down.

**Sash:** *[Loudly]* It feels as if we've reached Mars.

**Ishan:** *[Calmly]* I can hear you now. You can stop shouting.

As it was so silent, they started whispering to each other.

**Sash:** *[Whispering]* We have very little time. How can we find Sarthak?

**Ishan:** *[Puzzled]* I have no idea. Can you see all these souls of dead beings?

**Sash:** *[Nervously]* Yes, I'm scared. Baba didn't tell us anything about how we can find Sarthak.

**Ishan:** *[Remembering]* Wait, the messenger told you he was crying out loud. When he came to your house, he was crying out loud, and Baba told us to follow the sound. Follow the crying sound, Sash.

**Sash:** Wait, you're right.

**Ishan:** *[Noticing]* I think we're the only ones talking. There is silence all around. The moment he said that a bunch of animals started moving towards them.

**Ishan:** *[Panicking]* Sash, I don't know if it's true, but I read somewhere that we cannot allow souls to touch us. We might become like them.

**Sash:** Ishan, those are zombies. Those are fictional. This is reality.

**Ishan:** Oh, yaa... Okay *[Determined]* Listen, you go towards the right. I'll go towards the left. We have very little time left. We need to find Sarthak, and if you find him, ask him if he was talking about the necklace and where it is now.

**Sash:** Ok, done.

They both moved in opposite directions, walking quickly unlike the others so those animals won't touch them. Ishan felt someone grab his hand. He turned and saw a woman wearing a light blue gown. Her eyes widened when she saw Ishan. She became teary and said, "My baby..."

For the first time in his life, Ishan felt warmth and comfort, though in the coldest place he had ever been.

**Ishan:** *[Amazed]* Who are you?

**Shirley:** *[Softly]* I am Shirley, your mother. I died while giving birth to you, my son.

Ishan felt terrible, tears rolling down his eyes. This was the first time he had seen her and felt a mother's touch.

**Ishan:** *[Emotional]* Mom. I love you. Please come back, mom.

**Shirley:** I am here. You can stay with me.

**Ishan:** *[Resolute]* No, Mom, I am not dead. I am here to help a friend, to find someone.

**Shirley:** *[Concerned]* Are you serious? Don't let me go all mommy over you. Go back from wherever you have come. This is not the right place.

Ishan smiled, experiencing for the first time how a mother's anger feels.

**Ishan:** *[Pleading]* Mom, I promise I will go back, but could you please help me find Sarthak? He is crying somewhere here. We don't have much time. Please, Mom.

**Shirley:** *[Sorrowful]* We are free souls. No one knows each other here.

**Ishan:** *[Desperate]* Okay, but have you heard someone cry here?

**Shirley:** Yes, if you go towards my right-hand side, you will find a hill. There, I heard people crying. Lots of people were crying. Come, I'll take you.

She held his hand and led him towards the hill while he was wondering the whole time about his father's whereabouts. When they reached the hill, Ishan saw many people crying. Since he had barely seen Sarthak before, his only option was to yell, "Sarthak!"

A handsome man with sharp features approached him, his lips sealed. Ishan felt as if he had met him somewhere.

**Ishan:** Are you Sarthak?

The man nodded affirmatively.

**Ishan:** *[Pressing on]* Does K.N.I.F.E. mean you want the necklace to stay in the family? Again, Sarthak nodded.

**Ishan:** Where is the necklace?

The man started miming as if writing something. Ishan was baffled.

**Ishan:** *[Confused]* What?

Sarthak repeated the action. Ishan remained perplexed. Shirley intervened urgently.

**Shirley:** *[Urgently]* Son, go back. The doors might close soon.

She pulled Ishan away from Sarthak and guided him to the door. He turned back for a final look.

**Ishan:** *[Worried]* Mom, I still need to ask him a lot of questions.

**Shirley:** *[Hastily]* You cannot stay here. Please go before the door closes and live your life, son.

**Ishan:** *[Sad]* Okay but where is Dad?

**Shirley:** *[Surprised]* Why are you asking this? He's alive. What did he name you? When I was pregnant, I told him if it's a boy, we'll name him Shaun.

**Ishan:** *[Solemnly]* Dad is dead, Mom. I'm an orphan. I grew up in an orphanage. My name is Ishan.

**Shirley:** *[Shocked]* No, son, he's alive. He lives near...
The wind began to whistle in the opposite direction.

**Shirley:** *[Urgently]* Ishan, the doors might close.

**Ishan:** *[Desperate]* Where does he live, Mom, please tell me.

**Shirley:** *[Rushed]* You will find out. Please go fast. Get out.

**Ishan:** *[Determined]* My friend is in here too. I need to find her first. Sash? Sash? Sash?

Ishan turned around for a last glimpse of his mother. She hugged him, and he kissed her. Tears rolled down his eyes.

**Ishan:** *[Crying]* Mom, come back please.

**Shirley:** *[Reassuring]* I cannot, son, but I promise I will be there whenever you need me. Stop crying, my love. See, I am closer to God, so I will ask Him to make all your wishes come true. I love you, my Ishan.

**Ishan:** *[Resolutely]* Mom, if going back means staying away from you, then I don't want to go back. I would stay here happily with you forever. Life is very tough in our world. I want to be with you.

**Shirley:** *[Softly, with a touch of regret]* My child, life is there to live. *[Reflectively]* When we are alive, we waste our time thinking about stupid stuff, worrying what people would think and then when death comes, we feel as if we should have lived a little more. *[Encouragingly]* You live your life on your terms and no matter, in what situation you are, don't accept failure. *[Gently but firmly]* Don't think about what people would say, do whatever you feel is right but that doesn't mean you murder someone. *[With a hint of humour]* I just mean live, love and enjoy little moments. LOVE YOUR LIFE, SON.

*[Reassuringly]* Life is going to be like a wave but trust me you do not need a straight line.

Ishan was just staring at her as a little child does when they first see a rainbow. *[In awe and wonder]* He had always read in books and heard people talk about their moms. He was proud that as of today, he could also talk about his mother, but he was sad that he is going to miss her.

**Shirley:** *[Tenderly]* Don't be sad, son. *[Reassuringly]* I promise when your time comes, I will come to take you. *[With finality]* Now I will leave. I love you, Ishan.

**Ishan:** *[Voice trembling with emotion]* I love you too, Mom. I love you. I love you. I love you. I love you.

In this universe, Ishan lived both the moments of happiness and sadness. He realized everything is temporary. He was very happy that he got to meet his mom but couldn't stop his tears when he saw his mom go away. *[Heartbroken as he watched her fade]* She was moving farther and farther into infinity.

**Sash:** *[Urgently, searching]* Ishan? Ishan? Ishan?

**Ishan:** *[Reassuringly]* I am here.

**Sash:** *[Panicking, concerned]* Ishan, I couldn't find Sarthak. The doors are closing. I can't leave without him. *[Noticing Ishan's distress]* Why are you crying? Are you okay?

**Ishan:** *[With a mix of urgency and sadness]* I met my mom and I found Sarthak, talked to him. Let's jump outside.

**Sash:** *[Confused and anxious]* Your mom?

**Ishan:** *[Determined]* I will tell you everything later. Let's go outside first.

They tried to jump but couldn't.

**Ishan** *(panicking)*: *[Frantically]* What's happening? Why can't we go outside?

**Sash:** *[Pragmatically]* Ishan, I have no idea. Let's just find another way to go out otherwise, we would be stuck inside forever.

**Ishan:** *[Desperately]* Let's try to jump again.

They tried and still couldn't go out of that clock. They were scared.

**Sash:** *[With a sense of urgency]* Ishan, we need to take Hari with us. I promised him. I think that's the only way we'll be able to leave. Promises matter here, especially after you take an oath standing on a crow.

**Ishan** *[frustratedly, exasperated]* Why do you do these things? When did this happen? Okay, forget the details and find Hari.

Sayesha pondered how she met Hari outside the clock but now they seemed to be stuck inside.

**Ishan:** *[Seeking clarity]* What does Hari look like?

**Sash:** *[Defeated]* No, Ishan. Hari's outside. I don't know why we can't get out. I think we're trapped.

**Ishan:** Not possible. There must be a way.

**Sash:** *[Frustrated, overwhelmed]* I cannot think in such situations.

**Ishan:** *[Determined, with a theory]* I think I've figured it out. We'll have to leave the same way we entered. When the doors close, they throw out the unwanted souls.

**Sash:** *[Curious]* How do you know this?

**Ishan:** *[Speculatively]* I have no idea; I'm just trying to make sense of it. The clock didn't suck us in, it just sucked the dead animals and dead people, so I don't think it'll let us stay back in. Let's turn around. Keep your back to the entrance and face towards this red planet or whatever it is.

**Sash:** *[Agreeing]* Okay. Let's try this as well.

They turned around on the count of three. "One... Two... Three..."

They were thrown back from the door towards the outside. *[With a sudden rush]* Once again, the bell-like sound enveloped them, making them unable to hear each other. *[Holding onto each other for support]* They held hands tightly as they were propelled away.

# Tong, tong, tong

Tong, tong, tong

Tong, tong, tong

Tong, tong, tong

Tong, tong, tong

Tong, tong, tong

Tong, tong, tong

Tong, tong, tong

Tong, tong, tong

Tong, tong, tong

Tong, tong, tong

Tong, tong, tong

Tong, tong, tong

Tong, tong, tong

Tong, tong, tong

Tong, tong, tong

Tong, tong, tong

**Ishan:** *[Determined]* Okay, now tell me what you want to ask?

**Sash:** *[Curious]* What did Sarthak say?

**Ishan:** *[Confidently]* I was right, and I'll tell you more later. Let's go back to our bodies now. We have very little time. It's already 35 minutes.

**Sash:** *[Surprised]* You were counting?

**Ishan:** I looked at the time when we came out of that clock. It was 3:45am.

**Sash:** *[Calculating]* So, we have around 8-10 minutes to go back.

**Ishan:** *[Nodding]* Yes.

**Sash:** *[Urgently]* We have to take Hari back.

**Ishan:** *[Concerned]* Where is he now?

**Sash:** *[Calling out]* Hari? Hari? Hari? I think we'll have to look for him.

**Ishan:** *[Frustrated]* Why are you always attracting problems, Sash?

**Sash:** *[Regretfully]* He was not allowing me to move. He held my legs, or did he just put my legs over that dead crow because he wanted to go back? There is no such thing as an ALIVE SOUL. All souls are alive, that's why they are souls. Oh God! What did I do?

**Ishan:** *[Speculatively]* Maybe he wants to punish you by trapping you here.

**Sash:** *[Resolute]* Ishan, you go back. I will stay here.

**Ishan:** *[Alarmed]* Are you out of your mind? I cannot go without you because Baba entangled our spirits with that ritual. Do you remember?

**Sash:** *[Desperately]* Good God! What have I done?

Both of them sat on a big rock, trying to think of how they could get back. *[Worried]* "What if they couldn't return? What if they had the same fate as Hari?" *[Panicked]* Suddenly, they heard a voice calling, "Sayesha...

Sayesha..." They turned around and saw Hari standing right behind them. *[Relieved but anxious]*

## Chapter - 7
# HARI'S SKULLDUGGERY

**Hari:** *[Desperately]* You cannot leave without me. I need a vessel now. You must take me with you and give me one of your bodies to live in. I don't want to wander alone.

**Sash:** *[Confused]* A vessel?

**Hari:** Yes, I want to go back to complete my unfinished business. I cannot return to my body.

**Sash:** *[Puzzled]* Your body is still lying there, unburnt. Why can't you go back to it?

**Hari:** *[Frustrated]* I need a functioning body, you fool.

**Ishan:** *[Impatiently]* We have a few minutes left. Do whatever he asks, Sash. *[Looking at Hari]* I'll give you my body as a vessel.

**Sash:** *[Pleading]* Ishan, please, you cannot do this.

**Ishan:** *[Firmly]* Sash, seriously? This is not the time to discuss this. He won't let us go otherwise.

**Sash:** Okay, how can we take you?

**Hari:** *[Instructing]* Hold my hand and pull me towards you when you enter that circle.

**Ishan:** *[Confused]* What circle?

**Hari:** *[Explaining]* You must travel across the lake to find a circular structure that emits green light. You need to jump into that circle, and you will reach back to your bodies.

**Ishan:** *[Concerned]* The lake full of bodies...? How will we cross it?

**Hari:** *[Warns]* The lake looks calm, but the moment anyone touches it, it becomes turbulent. Waves come from both sides to pull you in. You need to step on the bodies and cross it. The lake is designed to absorb all the dead bodies. I failed to cross it, so I got stuck here.

**Sash:** *[Worried]* But if you failed, how do you know there's a circle emitting green light?

**Hari:** *[Regretful]* When I tried to cross the lake, I was just a few seconds late. I managed to pull myself out, but the circle became so small that I couldn't go through it, and I got stuck here. It gives you twenty-four hours to complete your task, or you'll be here forever. I waited for the next day, but I was attacked by birds and crows. A huge lizard choked me from behind, and by the time I reached the circle, it closed. I've been here ever since.

**Ishan:** *[Urgently]* We have three minutes left, Sash. We need to run.

**Sash:** *[Determined]* Let's go.

They ran towards the lake. When they reached near the lake, Ishan offered to go first. Hari jumped onto his shoulders, and Ishan held Sayesha's hand. The lake was red, full of blood and foul-smelling. It wasn't easy for a human to cross. They covered their noses, and as soon as Ishan stepped onto the first body, the lake's anger was evident. Waves started forming from far away, getting closer. They ran as fast as they could. As they were about to reach the other side, the waves hit Ishan, who began to drown. Sayesha and Hari immediately jumped across the lake.

She tried to pull Ishan, but he was sinking fast. In a flash of inspiration, she removed the cloth binding their hands and touched their wounds, entangling their souls. The moment she did this and pulled Ishan, he emerged from the lake.

The other side of the lake was bright and green, like a beautiful wonderland. Dark green trees, butterflies, blooming flowers, and soothing sounds brought a sense of calm they hadn't felt in a long time.

**Ishan:** *[Breathing heavily]* Wow, how did you do that?

**Sash:** *[Recollecting]* Remember, Baba said, "Your wounds are the key to this universe." I now understand the reason.

**Ishan:** I am proud of you. Thank you.

**Hari:** *[Urgently]* Let's run, or the circle will close.

Ishan got up from the ground, and they both ran towards the green light in the distance. They were shocked to see there was no circle around. The green light was emitting from a huge creature that looked like a strange, green-coloured lizard with legs so long they touched the ground while the lizard was on top of a tree. Both were astonished.

**Ishan:** *[Desperately searching]* Where is the circle?

**Hari:** *[Smiling]* I brought fresh meat, Sir.

Ishan and Sayesha couldn't understand.

**Sash:** *[Confused]* Why did you bring us here?

**Hari:** *[Explaining]* He is the king of this place and only eats fresh meat. He is angry now because he has been hungry for weeks. He was about to eat me when I first came here, but I promised to bring him fresh meat, so he spared my soul. Since then, whenever someone comes here, I bring them to him.

**Sash:** *[Worried]* So, there is no way we could go back?

**Hari:** *[Smiling]* There was. It was right above the rock you sat on.

**Ishan:** *[Surprised]* How didn't we see that?

**Hari:** *[Sighing]* It only opens when you sit on that rock with your legs crossed. When I saw you there, I thought you were about to leave, but I didn't know Baba hadn't told you about the way out when he sent you in. So, I deceived you and brought you here.

**Sash:** *[In disbelief]* Why did Baba do that?

**Ishan:** *[Frustrated]* I have no idea. Let's go back then.

**Hari:** *[Mockingly]* Do you think I am a fool? It's not easy going back there. The lake does not allow people from this place to go to the other side. You are trapped, just like me.

**Ishan:** *[Desperate]* How come you were there, then?

**Hari:** *[Soberly]* I am dead, Ishan. You still have your heart beating. Souls can travel anywhere.

**Ishan:** *[Begging]* Please help us.

They both looked behind when they felt a shadow; it was the huge lizard. The lizard had big eyes that looked like globes, green scaly skin, and a smile on its face.

**Ishan:** *[Urgently]* Run, Sash.

They started running towards the lake, and Hari ran behind them. When they reached the lake, they felt as if someone pushed them back. They couldn't even enter the lake.

**Hari:** *[Menacingly]* You have twenty-four hours, just like I had. Leave, if you can, or get ready to surrender yourselves.

Both tried harder and harder to go back to the lake but failed every time. They saw the lizard walking towards them, astonished to see it walking on two legs. They ran as fast as they could into the jungle but saw bats and birds flying above them, trying to encircle them. They waved their hands to shoo them away, but it was useless. Hari followed them all along. The deeper they went into the jungle, the more humid it became. They found a beautiful blue sea with lots of shells instead of sand. They threw the shells at the birds and bats following them. They heard a large echo which kept on increasing.

Hahhhhhhhhhhhhhhhhh...
Hahhhhhhhhhhhhhhhhh...
Hahhhhhhhhhhhhhhhhh...
Hahhhhhhhhhhhhhhhhh...

Hahhhhhhhhhhhhhhhhh...
Hahhhhhhhhhhhhhhhhh.
Hahhhhhhhhhhhhhhhhh....
Hahhhhhhhhhhhhhhhhhh....
Hahhhhhhhhhhhhhhhhhh......
Hahhhhhhhhhhhhhhhhhh....
Hahhhhhhhhhhhhhhhhhh......
Hahhhhhhhhhhhhhhhhhh......
Hahhhhhhhhhhhhhhhhhh......
Hahhhhhhhhhhhhhhhhhh....
Hahhhhhhhhhhhhhhhhhh......

Hahhhhhhhhhhhhhhh....

# Hahhhhhhhhhhhhhh....
# Hahhhhhhhhhhhhhh.....

It was the lizard, coming closer and closer. Ishan threw a big shell at its tail. *[Hoping for a distraction]* It screamed louder, but to his surprise, its tail repaired itself in minutes. Sayesha knew lizards were scared of water. *[Determined to use her knowledge]* She held Ishan's hand and dipped into the water. The lizard screamed louder and louder. Hari ran towards them.

They swam in the water for half an hour and found a small island-like structure nearby. Both of them went there.

They sat down under a tree. Sayesha started crying. *[Overwhelmed with guilt]*

**Sash:** *[Sobbing]* This is all because of me. I should not have done that. I am sorry, Ishan. Please find a way to go back. Please.

Ishan didn't say a word. He knew Hari also wanted to go back, so why not trick Hari into telling them the way back?

Ishan called out to him.

**Ishan:** *[Strategically]* Hari, if you tell us the way back to our universe, we will give your daughter the necklace that will make her rich.

**Hari:** *[Doubtful]* There is no such thing.

**Ishan:** *[Confidently]* Don't you know the necklace is the whole reason you are here, and we are here? It has miraculous powers. We know your daughter needs money.

**Sash:** *[Pleading]* Don't you love your daughter, Hari? If it were my father, he would do anything for me. You know she misses you.

**Ishan:** *[Insistent]* Also, once you enter my body, you can directly talk to her. We promise to help. You said we cannot break a promise made here.

**Hari:** *[Skeptical]* There is no dead crow here.

**Ishan:** *[Reassuringly]* I know this is heaven, Hari. Everything is pure here, and if we don't keep a promise made here, we will suffer the consequences.

**Hari:** This is not heaven.

**Ishan:** *[Assertively]* It sure looks like it.

**Hari:** *[Suspiciously]* How can I trust you?

**Sash:** *[Persuasively]* You will have to, Hari. This way, you can meet your daughter and make her rich. You could be with her forever if Ishan's body is alive. A true father breaks all the laws and suffers all the consequences just to make their daughter smile. Can't you do that?

**Hari:** *[Reluctantly]* Okay, I accept your terms. But if you don't give me what I want, I will kill Ishan.

**Ishan:** *[Firmly]* We promise. Now please tell us the way to go back.

**Hari:** *[Giving in]* There is only one way to go back. "Your wounds are the only way back."

**Ishan:** *[Confused]* What does that mean?

**Hari:** *[Explaining]* You will have to put your hands in this lake. It will suck your blood. The more blood it sucks, the weaker you will get, but the longer path will be formed for you to travel back. You both must put your hands in it together as your souls are entangled.

**Sash:** *[Concerned]* If you knew this, how come you did not come back?

**Hari:** *[Regretfully]* I had no wound, hence no blood. Also, my body was at the Tantric's house. Unless he could have helped make a wound, I would have escaped, but no communication was possible. Most importantly I did not know that when I came here first.

They moved back silently towards the lake. *[Trying to avoid the lizard]* They waited for a while and then swam across the sea to reach the forest. When they entered, there was silence all around. They slowly moved towards the lake. They were about to reach when they saw the lizard waiting for them near the lake.

**Ishan:** *[Worried]* How can we go there?

**Sash:** *[Whispering]* We will have to wait till he goes back.

**Ishan:** *[Concerned]* Do you think we have that much time left?

**Sash:** *[Hesitant]* I lost track of time. I just knew when we entered here that we had 24 hours. I don't know how much more time we have. Can't we just silently go there?

**Ishan:** *[Strategically]* Rather than walking, let's crawl slowly.

They started crawling towards the lake. The lizard was sleeping. As they reached the lake, Sayesha saw the lizard's eyes open and yelled, "Run, Ishan!" The lizard came closer and closer.

**Ishan:** *[Urgently]* On the count of three. One… Two… Three…

They both dipped their hands into the lake and saw a path forming from one side to the other. The fresh blood collected in the lake and created a path. They felt weak.

The lizard started running towards them, but he was so huge that he could not run fast. The land started moving and blood started splashing out.

Once the path was complete, they removed their hands and tried to get up but were unable to. They pushed themselves up and crawled along the path. Hari followed them.

In the present universe, the Tantric saw both their bodies turning pale. The rest of the gang started to worry.

Ishan and Sayesha crossed the path, finally reaching the other side. They tried to get up and go towards the rock. They knew the time Baba gave them had ended long ago, so they were trapped for a few more hours until the full 24 spare hours were completed. They went and sat on the rock. *[Feeling hopeless]* They had to wait a few more hours for the door to open, but to their surprise, the moment they crossed their legs, a big blue ray shone from above. It was so bright that they had to close their eyes. They felt their bodies getting heavier. Hari saw their bodies moving upwards, so he jumped and sat on Ishan's shoulder. Ishan was disturbed.

Baba continued to chant mantras all along, but now he was chanting faster and louder. *[Panicked]* He could feel the flame going down. All the other members of the squad were afraid. They prayed for Sayesha and Ishan to wake up fast. As the flame started going down, Nisha saw their bodies moving. *[Excited]* She yelled, "They are back!" Ava and Kush were sitting on the floor as their chairs broke during the mantras. Ava even hurt her ankle. Kush was bleeding from a shattered window's glass. All of them did not move at all, as advised by Baba Ji.

The flame went out, and both of them opened their eyes. Baba saw something weird in Ishan's eye but did not say a word. All of them were relieved and hugged both of them while Baba Ji looked sad as if he didn't want both of them to come back.

**Ishan:** *[in a very dull tone, confused]* What happened to you guys?

**Kush:** *[Trying to reassure]* It's okay. Nothing happened. We are fine. These twenty-four hours were the hardest time of my life.

**Ava:** *[Pointing out]* Where is Sash running to?

**Ishan:** *[Alarmed]* She cannot run; she is weak.

**Ava:** *[Insistent]* No, she is running. See…

**Nisha:** *[Concerned]* Why is she running towards the lake?

Ishan realized what Sayesha was about to do. *[Panicking]* He ran as fast as he could. Nisha, Ava, and Kush couldn't believe their eyes seeing how fast Ishan ran.

**Baba:** *[Gravely]* Someone has come up with Ishan.

**Ava:** *[Confused]* Means?

**Baba:** A soul is attached to Ishan's body.

**Nisha:** *[Shocked]* What??

While they were talking, Kush started the car and drove very fast, heading towards Ishan. He hit Ishan with his car, so he fell down, and so did Hari's soul. The rest of them ran towards the car. Kush had already realized what was going to happen. Ishan got up, but Kush tried to stop him. Ishan was so powerful now that he threw Kush far away and started running towards Sayesha. By the time he reached the lake, Sayesha had already started burning Hari's body.

Ishan yelled, cried, and fell to the ground. After a while, Baba arrived and put holy water on his body. They all witnessed something like a diffused flame going off from Ishan's body. All of them were tired and breathless from all the running, especially Sayesha. She was praised for the courage to run despite being so weak after coming from another universe.

They started talking in very low tones.

**Ava:** *[Proudly]* I am proud of you, Sash.

**Sash:** *[Concerned]* Are you okay, Ishan?

**Ishan:** *[Reassured]* Yes. Where is Kush?

**Nisha:** *[Pointing]* He is over there.

They ran towards him only to find out he was alive but had broken ribs. Baba asked them to take Kush to the hospital as there was no other ritual left.

**Sash:** *[Gratefully]* Thank you once again, Baba Ji, for your help.

**Baba:** *[Solemnly]* You have paid for your sins. God bless you all.

## Chapter - 8
## SECRETS AND LIES

The whole squad took Kush to the hospital and called his parents. When the doctor inquired about how he got injured, Ishan explained that Kush had an accident near the highway. Kush's parents were worried and furious with everyone for going on a drive so early in the morning. Kush was taken to the operation theatre because he was having difficulty breathing and needed immediate attention. All of them waited anxiously outside.

**Ava:** *[Gently]* How are you both?

**Ishan:** *[Nodding, trying to stay composed]* We're okay. *[With a distant look]* Something miraculous happened when I was in there.

**Ava:** *[Curious]* Where?

**Ishan:** *[Looking off, lost in thought]* When we went inside that clock-shaped structure.

**Sash:** *[Concerned]* What happened?

**Ishan:** *[Voice wavering]* I met my mom.

**Sash:** *[Softly, trying to offer comfort]* Yes, I remember you telling me that when you were crying. Maybe it was an illusion. I felt disoriented too. It felt like I was running but getting nowhere.

**Ishan:** *[Firmly]* Sash, this is about me for once. I really met my mom. Her name was Shirley. I cried in there. She also told me my father is alive.

**Sash:** *[Sympathetically]* I'm sorry. Did she tell you where he lives?

**Ishan:** *[Frustrated]* She was about to, but the door started closing, so we jumped out.

**Nisha:** *[In awe]* Oh my God. Maybe you met your mom for a reason.

**Ishan:** *[tearing up, emotional]*: I don't know, but those were the best moments of my life. She touched me, you know.

**Nisha:** *[Gently]* Don't cry, Ishan.

**Ishan:** *[Puzzled and hurt]* Why did my father leave me in the orphanage?

**Sash:** *[Reassuringly]* Ishan, we will find out. Let's get an update on Kush's condition first, then we'll investigate it.

**Ishan:** *[Determined]* No, once Kush is fine, let's finish your matter first.

**Sash:** *[Resolutely]* Hmm.

After long hours of surgery, Kush was in stable condition but still unconscious. His parents told the squad to go home and rest, as they must be exhausted after a long night. Ishan hesitated, but Ava convinced him, reminding them that they needed to meet Sarthak's mom soon, as there was little time left.

**Ishan:** Okay, uncle, we'll leave now. Please let us know once Kush wakes up; we'll come back to the hospital.

**Kush's Dad:** *[Nodding]* Sure, son. Will do.

**Nisha:** *[Concerned]* Ava, don't you have to meet your daughter?

**Ava:** *[Reassuringly]* No, Raunak will handle her. I told him about Kush's accident, so he thinks we are at the hospital.

This time, Ishan drove while Sayesha gave directions to Sarthak's house. When they neared the building, Ishan experienced déjà vu. He felt like he had been there before.

**Sash:** *[Casually]* The building is in the city center, so you might have passed by it many times.

**Ishan:** *[Frowning, confused]* No, I distinctly remember coming here for something. I know there's a huge Star Wars poster in the lobby.

**Sash:** *[Nodding]* Yes, there is. But when did you come here?

**Ishan:** *[Struggling to recall]* I'm forgetting that.

As they pressed the elevator button for the 18th floor, Nisha marveled.

**Nisha:** Wow, this is an amazing place. Sarthak must have been rich.

**Ava:** Of course, he was. He had that necklace that made every wish come true.

**Nisha:** *[Curious]* Yes, I want to know the whole story behind that necklace.

They rang the bell of penthouse No. 1802. The nameplate read "Mrs. Shimona Roy." Their housekeeper, Raghu, opened the door.

**Raghu:** *[Politely]* Yes, sir? Who do you want to meet?

**Ishan:** *[Firmly]* We want to meet Sarthak's mother, Mrs. Shimona.

**Raghu:** *[Curiously]* Who are you?

**Ishan:** We are his friends. We need to talk to her about something important related to him, in private.

**Raghu:** *[Nodding]* Okay. She is in a meeting right now. You might have to wait for 10-15 minutes.

**Ava:** *[Reassuringly]* Sure, we have no issues.

**Raghu:** *[With a hint of recognition]* Ahh... please don't mind me asking, but you are Nisha, right

**Nisha:** *[Surprised]* Yes, how do you know me?

**Raghu:** *[Smiling]* Sarthak sir talked about you a lot.

**Nisha:** *[Incredulous]* He knew me?

**Raghu:** *[Nodding]* Yes, he was your husband's colleague. Adesh Sir used to come here often.

**Nisha:** *[Puzzled]* Really? He never told me. But how do you know I am his wife?

**Raghu:** *[Invitingly]* Why don't you all come inside? I'll tell you everything. Please have a seat. I'll get some water for you all.

**Ava:** Thank you.

When Raghu went to fetch water, they admired the beautiful penthouse. They were seated in a luxurious, air-conditioned, double-height room with an extravagant Swarovski chandelier, a huge pearl-white couch, a large rectangular ceramic center table, and a massive mural art piece on the wall. The living room was so spacious it could easily accommodate around twenty people. The floor was covered with pure Italian marble tiles, with a beautiful antique rug beneath the center table.

**Ava:** *[Admiring]* Sash, did you see that carving on the wall? It's so beautiful.

**Sash:** *[Nodding]* Yes, I noticed it the last time I was here. You should see their washroom. It's like in the movies, with a huge bathtub and speakers.

**Ava:** *[Impressed]* Wow... here comes Raghu Kaka.

**Raghu:** *[Handing over water]* Here, please have some water.

**Nisha:** *[Curious]* Thank you. You were telling me how you know me.

**Raghu:** *[Hesitant]* Please don't tell Shimona madam.

**Ava:** *[Reassuring]* We won't.

**Raghu:** *[Confiding]* I have been working here since Sarthak was born. We became friends over the years. He used to tell me about his girlfriends and friends. One day, Mr. Adesh came home with Sarthak. They were drinking in Sarthak's room. No one else was home, so they called me to join them. While talking, Adesh showed us a picture of you. Then they did something very bad that night.

**Nisha:** *[Urgently]* What did they do?

**Raghu:** *[Pleading]* Please, don't tell anyone.

**Nisha:** *[Firmly]* We won't. Just tell me what they did.

**Raghu:** *[Recounting]* Adesh told Sarthak about a beautiful friend of his wife named Sash. He even showed him a picture. I didn't see it, but Sarthak did. They were so drunk that they made a fake social media profile under the name Raj and sent a friend request to her. She accepted it, and they started chatting. Sarthak found her interesting and asked to meet, but she declined, saying they should get to know each other first. Sarthak had a short temper, and this was the first time he faced rejection. So, he took her pictures from her profile, edited them, and posted them online as nudes.

**Nisha:** *[Shocked]* What??? So, he was the guy who stalked Sash. Sash, remember we all tried to find Raj but couldn't?

**Ishan:** *[Realizing]* Yes, I remember everything now.

**Ava:** *[Confused]* What?

**Sash:** *[Disappointed]* I never said I wouldn't meet him. I just told him we should get to know each other first. I never expected he would do something like this over a stupid rejection.

**Ishan:** *[Explaining]* It wasn't just about your rejection. I remember how I know this building. Kush reported Raj to the police. When they came here, they couldn't find Raj because his real name was Sarthak. He thought you reported him and intimidated Adesh. Adesh got scared because Raj was not only his colleague, but his mother owned the company. Raj forced him to get your number, but Adesh knew if he gave it, there would be a war since your father is a renowned man. So instead, he gave Kush's number. Adesh then called Kush and told him the whole story. Kush told me, and we were waiting for Raj's call. After one or two days, Raj, drunk, called Kush, who pretended to be you. Raj told him to drop the case for money. We agreed on one condition: we needed the money first. Raj asked us to meet him at his place.

When he came downstairs to escort Sash, he found both of us instead. Kush beat him up. Raj yelled that he would make your life a living hell.

**Sash:** *[Regretfully]* I told you guys not to involve the police.

**Ishan:** *[Regretfully]* I know, but Kush's uncle is in the CBI, so we did everything discretely. He was the one who took down your pictures and that stupid page. When I met Sarthak in that... hell or whatever it was, I felt like I had seen him somewhere before. But we didn't have much time, so I didn't think about it.

**Sash:** *[Frustrated]* Everything happening to me is because of you guys. When Sarthak told my uncle his name was Raj, I was worried. But I never thought he was the same guy. That's why he's haunting me. When people die, they come to know the truth, at least that's what I have heard. So why is he torturing me and not Kush?

**Ishan:** *[Sympathetically]* Kush is already in the hospital, Sash. And we don't know what happens when someone dies. I just know their soul comes back if they have unfinished business. This too I have only read in books and seen in movies.

**Sash:** This is so bad. He has literally made my life a living hell. He's taking advantage of my innocence.

**Ishan:** *[Angrily]* You're not innocent, Sash. You've done a lot of things that led us here. Why did you say yes to help him when you went to that psychic lady?

**Nisha:** *[Calming]* Guys... guys... don't fight, please. Whatever happened was wrong, but we have to handle everything maturely now.

**Ava:** *[Agreeing]* Yes.

**Raghu:** *[Apologetically]* I'm sorry about what happened to you, Sayesha ma'am. The last time you came to the house, I didn't know you were Sash. I don't know what's happening with you now, but I promise to help if you need me. Shh... ma'am is coming.

**Shimona:** *[Entering]* Hello. I'm sorry to keep you waiting. I was stuck in a meeting.

**Nisha:** *[Respectfully]* It's okay, aunty.

**Shimona:** I prefer to be called ma'am, not aunty.

Nisha: *[Apologetically]* Sorry, ma'am.

**Shimona:** *[Politely]* It's alright. Please, tell me what I can do for you.

**Sash:** *[Seriously]* Ma'am, I have something very important to tell you.

**Shimona:** *[Dismissively]* Oh, Sayesha. How many times do I have to tell you my son is dead? You must have seen someone else. Also, there is no garden in that hospital.

**Sash:** *[Firmly]* I know, ma'am. It was a graveyard just outside and to the right of the hospital. It's so beautifully developed that we mistook it for a garden. But there's something else. I want to ask if you know about a family necklace that makes wishes come true.

**Shimona:** *[Laughing]* We have many family necklaces made of gold, diamond, even silver, but none of them have powers. If you didn't study as a child, let me tell you, non-living things don't have magical powers, dear. Those are all fictional.

**Sash:** *[Desperately]* Ma'am, this is not a joke. Sarthak's soul has been haunting me for two years over that necklace.

**Shimona**: *[Turning to the others]* Either this girl needs money, or she is mentally unstable. I think the latter is true because I know my son was so handsome that any girl would go mad after falling in love with him. Please take her to a psychiatrist.

**Ishan:** *[Apologetically]* I'm sorry if we hurt your feelings, ma'am, but what she's saying is true.

**Shimona**: *[Angrily]* Look Sir, if my son wanted something, he would have come to me, not her. He loved me. You all think this is a joke, but I lost a son. You will not understand how difficult it is to handle such a loss. Just because I'm sitting here talking to you doesn't mean I'm fine. I have a family to feed. I have another son, a daughter, and a mother-in-law. They lost a family member too, and I'm here to make them strong. So, you better shut your mouths and leave. I can't entertain you anymore.

**Ava:** *[Apologetically]* I'm sorry, ma'am. We'll leave now.

**Shimona**: *[Dismissively]* Yes, please.

As they were about to leave, an old lady entered. She was furious to see Shimona so angry. She looked at Raghu and said, "Who are these kids, and why are they making my daughter- in-law angry?"

**Raghu:** *[Explaining]* Ani Maa, they're saying Sarthak's soul talked to them about some necklace he wants.

**Ani Amma**: *[Firmly]* Listen, children, we have been through a lot, and you are all delusional. So please, leave us alone.

**Nisha:** *[Inquisitively]* And you are?

**Ani Amma:** *[Furiously]* I am Sarthak's grandmother, Anindita Roy.

**Ava:** *[Apologetically]* I'm sorry, ma'am. Let's go, guys.

They all apologized and left Sarthak's house. They had no clue what to do next. They decided to go to a coffee shop near the building to give themselves time to think about these events.

Ishan was confused and felt lost without Kush. He needed a man-to-man talk. They entered the coffee shop and ordered their favourites. The aroma of the coffee calmed them down, and they felt relaxed. They all had sandwiches to satisfy their hunger.

**Ava:** *[Dialing her phone]* I'm calling Kush's mom to ask about him.

**Ishan:** *[Nodding]* Yes, go ahead.

Ava called and learned that Kush was conscious now. They were all happy that he was in stable condition. They decided to visit him at the hospital after finishing their coffee. They drove to the hospital.

**Ishan:** *[Smiling]* Hey, buddy. How are you doing?

**Kush:** *[In a low voice]* I'm okay. Thanks for bringing me to the hospital in time.

**Ishan:** *[Grateful]* Thanks to you for saving my life. If you hadn't stopped me, Hari's soul would still be stuck with me.

**Kush:** *[Weakly]* It was Sash who got the strength and idea to burn his body. Otherwise, we all wouldn't be here.

**Sash:** *[Gently]* Please don't talk much, Kush. You need rest.

**Kush:** *[Trying to stay upbeat]* No, it's alright. I was getting bored anyway. I need some gossip. Nisha, start.

**Nisha:** *[Smiling]* Okay, so Ishan met his mom in another universe and learned his father is alive. We went to Sarthak's house, and he was the same man who edited Sash's pictures and posted them online.

**Kush:** *[Surprised]* Raj??

**Ishan:** *[Affirmatively]* Yes, man. He was the same guy, and that's why he's making Sash do his unfinished work.

**Sash:** *[Threateningly]* I will beat you up, Kush, for whatever you did earlier, once you're fine.

**Kush:** *[Jokingly]* Better beat me now while I still have some anaesthesia. It might not hurt as much.

They all laughed for the first time in two days.

**Kush:** *[Curiously]* So, what's the plan now?

**Ava:** *[Shrugging]* We have no idea. By the way Ishan met his mom in another world.

**Kush:** Wow... *[Inquiring]* How did you feel after meeting your mom, Ishan?

**Ishan:** As I have never felt before. You know she wanted to name me Shaun.

**Nisha:** *[Playfully]* Wow, such a sexy name. We will call you Shaun going forward.

**Ishan:** Haha, Sure.

**Kush:** *[Curious]* Sash, can I ask you something, if you don't mind?

**Sash:** *[Nodding]* Yes, Kush, sure.

**Kush:** *[Curiously]* You told us earlier that Sarthak visits you every night and you do a ritual to keep him from harming you. Then you said you felt pity for him because he cries when he comes. But you suddenly changed your story, saying he might not come every night, and you took us to that tantric.

**Ishan:** *[Agreeing]* Yes, true. Why didn't we think of this before? Sash, is there anything else you're hiding?

**Sash:** *[Sighing]* I killed a man, and ever since then, something strange happens to me every night around 3:00 am-3:30 am. I get these weird visions, which is why I perform that ritual.

**Ava:** *[Skeptical]* Bullshit. Do you think we're kids in kindergarten?

**Nisha:** *[Accusing]* She must, considering how she's been fooling us since we met.

**Sash:** Guys, please, trust me.

**Ishan:** *[Frustrated]* Yeah, we've trusted you more than we should since day one.

**Sash:** *[Annoyed]* Kush, seriously, why don't you just rest as you're supposed to? Fine, it's true that Sarthak visits me every night asking for the K.N.I.F.E. He might have come that night, but since we weren't there, he haunted me on our way to the Tantric's place. I saw him on the side of the road multiple times while we were driving, which is why I went blank a few times. Tantric Baba has a mark near his house that spirits can't cross.

*[With a tremble in her voice]* When Hari was killed because of my mistake, bad things started happening at Tantric's place. The lake near his house dried up, trees fell and damaged his home, and his ability to sense spirits diminished. He even had a paralysis attack. I paid for his hospitalization, but now his left leg doesn't work. As he lost his powers, he couldn't help people, and he ran out of food. He called me, saying he'd never made a mistake like he did that day by not warning Hari. I told him it was my fault, but he insisted it was his too. He's had these visions since childhood and learned "Tantra Vidya" to help people, but there's a condition: you can't harm anyone, and you can't ask for money. He could only eat the food his clients gave him. I offered him food, but he rejected it. He said I had to apologize to Hari in another universe and perform the rituals, or he'd hand me over to the police. That's why he didn't burn Hari's body; it would restore his powers after I paid for my sins.

*[Looking away, pained]* But if I went through with it, I might lose my life, so I needed another body to bring me back if I got stuck. I asked Ishan for help, getting his consent indirectly. Tantric gave me a month, or he'd go to the police. Then, one day I saw Ava in the park with her baby and planned to involve you all. I knew he loved cricket, so I purposely planned the party on the day of

match. As per my plan I sent Ishan to my room to watch TV, knowing he'd see my setup and offer to help. I let him win the game to make him see how vulnerable I was.

*[Voice breaking]* I knew this would happen, but I didn't expect Ishan to involve everyone. He is an orphan. If anything happened to him, no one will mind. I wasn't ready to tell you anything, but he forced me. He also solved the K.N.I.F.E. mystery, which will help us find the necklace to give to Sarthak, so he'll leave me alone. Then, I'll move to Chicago with my parents.

**Ava:** *[Angrily]* You're as evil as Sarthak, Sash. We're not helping you anymore. I can't believe you risked Ishan's life to repay your sins.

**Sash:** *[Desperately]* I planned to apologize to Hari, and come back, but he pulled me inside the clock then his stupid mother intervened, he met Sarthak and blah blah blah. I did not know he would actually find Sarthak.

**Ishan:** *[Hurt and resentful]* A mother always protects her child, even after death, Sash. You might have left me to die if you got a chance. I was the one who helped you get out of that clock-shaped structure. Instead of thanking me, you insult my mother.

**Nisha:** *[Firmly]* Ava's right, you're evil, Sash. Good luck with your endeavour, but we won't help you.

**Sash:** *[Resigned]* Ok fine. I'm sorry to bother you all. I think I should leave.

**Ava:** *[Coldly]* Bye.

Sayesha left the room, and the others began discussing what they had endured because of her. They were deeply disappointed. Ishan couldn't believe how rude Sayesha had been. Nisha, feeling hungry, asked if anyone else wanted to eat. They decided on sandwiches, but the food application was down. So, Nisha and Ava went to the hospital canteen to get something.

While returning, they saw Sayesha sitting on the stairs, crying. Nisha felt bad and told Ava, "Sash has only had a cup of coffee since morning. Maybe we should ask if she needs anything."

**Ava:** *[Indifferently]* Let her die. I don't care.

**Nisha:** *[Softly]* Ava, please. I know what she did was wrong, and I'll never trust her again, but we should ask if she wants something to eat. It's basic humanity.

They approached Sayesha, who wiped her tears and asked what they wanted now.

**Ava:** *[Gently]* You don't have to be so rude.

**Nisha:** *[Talking softly]* Sash, we got some sandwiches and pineapple juice. Do you want anything? You must be hungry.

Sayesha burst into tears at Nisha's kindness. She couldn't believe Nisha would be nice after everything she'd done.

**Sash:** *[Choked with emotion]* Why are you being so nice to me after I risked all of your lives for my selfish gain?

**Nisha:** *[Sympathetically]* We're just concerned. We don't trust you anymore, but it's about humanity.

**Sash:** *[Sobbing]* Thank you, Nisha. I'm really sorry for my behaviour. I've been so tense for the last two years that I can't live in peace. I don't even know if this is a life worth living. I was on the verge of suicide before I met you all. I know I trapped myself in this mess, but I don't know how to move on. I'm sorry, Ava. I'm sorry, Nisha. Please forgive me.

Ava, one of Sayesha's closest friends since childhood, felt a pang of empathy seeing Sayesha's condition. Sayesha had supported Ava through her abortion, depression, and a huge fight with her parents when they threw her out of their house for wanting to marry Raunak. Ava couldn't stop herself from hugging Sayesha. Nisha joined them in a hug.

**Sash:** *[Pleading]* Can I get a piece of sandwich? I'm very hungry.

**Ava:** *[Softening]* Yes, take the whole sandwich. We got an extra. Let's go to Kush's room together.

**Sash:** *[Reluctantly]* No, you guys go. Ishan is furious with me.

**Nisha:** *[Reassuringly]* Don't worry about him. I'll manage everything.

**Ava:** *[Encouragingly]* Yes, let's go.

All three went to Kush's room where Ishan was sitting. The moment he saw Sayesha, he got up and hugged her.

**Nisha:** *[Relieved]* I thought I'd have to convince Ishan, but he's fine.

**Sash:** *[Concerned]* What happened, Ishan? Is everything okay?

**Ishan:** *[Tense]* You didn't hear the news?

**Ava:** *[Curious]* What news?

**Ishan:** *[Urgently]* The bridge connecting your house to this road collapsed. Many people died. I thought you might have left the hospital and I got scared.

**Sash:** *[Panicked]* Oh my God, Ishan. Don't worry, I'm fine. I'm alright.

**Ishan:** *[Bitterly]* Yes, you always are since you throw your problems on others.

**Nisha:** *[Calmly]* Ishan, let it go. Don't be angry. Sash is already sorry for what she did. Let's forgive her.

**Sash:** *[Sincerely]* Ishan, Kush, I'm really sorry for my behaviour and what I did to you all. I know it's not easy to forgive me, but I promise I'll never hurt you again.

**Kush:** *[Weary]* It's ok. I don't have much to say, but I don't think I can trust you anymore.

**Ishan:** *[Firmly]* Me neither.

**Sash:** *[Resolutely]* It's alright. I will prove myself to you all. I am sorry again.

**Ishan:** *[Firmly]* We're not helping you anymore, keep that in mind.

**Sash:** *[Determined]* Yes, I will handle everything alone. Don't worry.

They all sat down and started eating when Nisha's phone rang. She picked up the call, and it turned out to be Sarthak's grandmother. When she asked what she wanted, his grandmother told her to bring the squad and meet her at the safehouse. She even gave the address. Nisha then told everyone, and they wondered how Sarthak's grandmother got Nisha's number.

**Ava:** *[Thoughtfully]* Remember, at the coffee shop we gave Nisha's number while billing? Either she got your number from there or she called Adesh.

**Ishan:** *[Skeptically]* How would she know we went to the coffee shop?

**Ava:** *[Uneasily]* I don't know, I just felt like someone was following us while we were there. Anyway, the question is, are we going to that safehouse?

**Sash:** *[Stubbornly]* No need. I will go by myself.

**Ishan:** *[Nodding]* Yes, good.

**Kush:** *[Firmly]* No, Sash. You cannot go alone. All of you, please go with her. I've had you all with me for two hours now, and I need rest. I'll sleep. Tell me tomorrow what happened.

**Ishan:** *[Defiantly]* I am not going with her.

**Ava:** *[Pleading]* Please, Ishan, let's go and at least see what that old lady wants to tell us. If it's something stupid, we can leave.

**Nisha:** *[Encouragingly]* Yes, Ishan. Please, let's go.

**Sash:** *[Imploring]* Guys, please. Let me handle this. You've done enough.

**Ishan:** *[Reluctantly]* I can't let you manipulate us anymore, but Ava is right, we need to see what she wants to say.

## Chapter - 9
## FROM GREED TO DEATH

After a lot of thinking, they all went to the place where Sarthak's grandmother had asked them to come. When they arrived, they found a small wooden house in the middle of a large park that looked like a jungle. Near the house was a lake, reminding Ishan of the lake he saw when he went to the other universe. The house looked dull, with a porch out front, two garden tables, and some chairs. Tall trees and creepers surrounded the house, giving it a beautiful yet spooky vibe. A cold wind was blowing, and the weather had shifted, hinting at an impending rainstorm. They were the only ones there. They waited for Ani Amma for half an hour, but she didn't show up.

**Ava:** *[Irritated]* Let's leave. I think that old bitch was playing with us.

**Nisha:** *[Pointing]* Look, there's a car coming.

The car stopped in front of the house. Ani Amma got out and looked at all of them.

**Ani Amma:** *[Authoritatively]* Come inside, it's going to rain.

They all went inside the house and sat in the living room. The room was spacious, but not as large as their penthouse. It had a brown carpet covering the floor, two wall fans, an old table in the corner, and small diwan seating instead of huge couches. The house felt cozy. Antique dream catchers made of wool threads adorned one wall, while a small bookshelf stood on the opposite side. Stairs led up on the left side of the room, with a small washroom beneath them. The ceiling was shaped like a hut. Pillows and blankets were scattered on the three diwan seats. They all settled in comfortably when Raghu walked in as well.

**Nisha:** *[Surprised]* Raghu? You here?

**Raghu:** *[Nodding]* Ani Amma brought me here.

**Ava:** *[Curious]* What happened, Ma'am? You wanted to tell us something?

**Ani Amma:** *[Warmly]* Please, you can call me Amma. This "mam" word seems very formal. Okay, so when you all came to my house, I heard what you said. I know you weren't lying, but my daughter-in-law has been through a lot, and she does so much for her children. I didn't want to scare her by telling her the things I'm going to tell you now.

**Ishan:** *[Reassuringly]* Yes, we understand. Please continue.

**Ani Amma:** *[Sighing]* I know which necklace you were talking about. Years ago, my husband and I lived in Konkan. We had a small farm where we grew grains and sold them. We were very poor. One day, it was raining heavily when a car stopped by our house. The man in the car was trying to start it again and again, but it didn't work. My husband felt bad for him and asked him to come inside to stay for the night. The man agreed as there was no other way to get back to his house in that heavy rain. I cooked dinner for both of them. The man had a bottle of whisky with him, so he offered it to us, and they both started drinking. The man was very rich. He got so drunk that night he told my husband he had a necklace that made wishes come true. My husband was shocked to hear that. Being greedy, he checked the man's car and bag while he was sleeping and stole the necklace. He didn't know how it worked, so he spent the whole night trying to figure it out. Around 4 am, the rich man woke up to go to the washroom and found out my husband had the necklace. They fought for a long time. My husband, being strong, twisted the man's neck, killing him on the spot. But while dying, he kept saying, 'K.N.I.F.E.'

**Ishan:** *[Astonished]* What? Really?

**Ani Amma:** *[Nodding, with a sober tone]* Yes. I woke up after I heard someone yell. When I came out of my room, I saw that man lying on the ground. We got scared, so we kept his bag with us and, before morning, dug a pit in our backyard and buried the body. *[Pauses, her voice trembling]* We went through his papers. His name was Adrian Mathews. We didn't know what to do with the car, so we threw it in the lake. *[Sighs]* We did it so discreetly that no one doubted us. There were no cell phones back then, so tracking was not easy. *[Looks down, reflecting]* But a few days later, a lady named Roma came searching for her husband. She was pregnant. The moment I saw her, I knew she was Adrian's wife. *[Voice softens with regret]* I wanted to tell her everything as I was feeling so guilty, but my husband never allowed me to. *[Shakes her head slightly]* We talked to her for a while, then she went back home. My husband asked me to make friends with her so we could crack the code on how the necklace worked. *[Gazes far away, remembering]* She was a beautiful and polite lady. She was so rich that I knew she would never be friends with me. *[Nods sadly]* So, we shifted to the city, and I went to her house to ask if she needed any house help. I requested so much that she agreed to keep me in her house. I worked there for months, and when she slept, I tried to investigate her cabinets to find the code. *[Looks apologetically]* One afternoon, when I was cooking lunch, her labour pain started. I took her to the hospital as she had no one else in her family apart from her mother-in-law, who was very old. *[Smiles faintly at the memory]* She gave birth to a beautiful baby girl who looked exactly like her father. While she was in the hospital, she told me she needed someone to take care of her mother-in-law, so I asked if my husband could do so. She agreed happily.

**Ani Amma:** *[With a touch of guilt]* My husband started working there, taking care of her mother-in-law and trying to find the code as well. *[Pauses, recalling]* There was a small storeroom in the house that was always locked. After Roma delivered the baby, she went into postpartum depression, so the doctor asked us to stay a few more days in the hospital. *[Sighs, a hint of tension in her voice]* One day, while I was at the hospital, my husband gave sleeping pills to Adrian's mom and broke the storeroom's door. *[Nods slowly, eyes clouded with remorse]* There he found a box with some notes and mantras. He knew he had found the code to activate the necklace.

**Ishan:** *[Sarcastically]* So, basically, your husband killed two people. Wow, you come from a family of serial killers. Sash is a good fit for your family.

**Ava:** *[Annoyed]* Shut up, Ishan.

**Sash:** *[Sincerely]* I am so sorry, Amma. You had to bear so much.

**Nisha:** *[Curious]* Amma was also part of the murder, right? She helped her husband.

**Ani Amma:** *[Defensively]* I had no choice but to help him after I saw him kill that man ruthlessly. I was scared he might kill me too. And yes, Adrian's mom didn't die. He just gave her an extra sleeping pill. When she woke up at night, she saw my husband repairing the door. He gave her some excuse, and she believed him. Thank God she did, otherwise, he would have killed her as well.

**Sash:** *[Concerned]* Did the necklace get activated?

**Ani Amma:** *[Nodding]* Yes, it did, after a few days of rituals, and we started getting money from various sources. We were happy. After a year, I delivered a boy, Samarth, Sarthak's father. We became so rich that we started our own company.

**Ishan:** *[Curious]* What happened to Roma then?

**Ani Amma:** Oh, I left the job, of course, because we were rich.

**Nisha:** *[Inquisitive]* Did you come to know what the meaning of K.N.I.F.E. was?

**Ani Amma:** *[Thoughtfully]* Those papers from that box Adrian hid clearly said the necklace should not be touched by a woman. *[Pausing, remembering the gravity of the warning]* It will fulfil all your wishes until it is used to destroy someone else's life. It had some mantras. *[Reflectively]* It also said one man could pass the necklace to another generation only if he has a baby boy. If he has a daughter, he must give the necklace to someone else or keep it in the family estate until his daughter gives birth to a baby boy. *[Sighing]* My husband fulfilled all his wishes, but one day we started experiencing business losses. *[With a hint of frustration]* He got furious and threw the necklace on the floor. It hit the floor so hard it opened. We never realized that the pendant was so thick because it had some paper in it, which revealed some truths. *[With a touch of regret]* This happened when Samarth, my son, was around 20 years old.

**Ishan:** *[Eager]* Wait. First, tell me how Adrian got that necklace and secondly, what did that paper reveal?

**Nisha:** *[Frustrated]* I am so confused. This is such a mess.

**Ava:** *[Resigned]* And now we are in it.

**Ani Amma:** I just know that Adrian's grandfather was gifted that necklace by a king who had it specially made for him as he did something good for the king.

Now, that paper revealed that if the necklace is given to someone, it has the power of returning to the original family estate once a son is born in the family. So basically, until there was no son, it worked. But the moment a son was born, the necklace stopped working.

**Ishan:** Oh my God, which means that Roma's daughter gave birth to a son.

**Ani Amma:** *[Laughing]* Hahaha... We thought the same, but Shirley was not pregnant. She wasn't even married then.

**Ishan:** *[Confused]* Shirley??

**Ani Amma:** *[Nodding]* Yes, Roma's daughter Shirley. Why, what happened?

**Nisha:** *[Calmly]* Nothing, Ishan's mother's name was also Shirley.

**Ani Amma:** *[Intrigued]* Really? What about your father?

**Ishan:** *[Shrugging]* I don't know anything about him. I am an orphan.

**Ani Amma:** *[Muttering]* Hmmmm... Okay, okay, okay.

**Ava:** *[Curious]* What happened?

**Ani Amma:** *[Sighing heavily]* Nothing. So yes, then our bad days started. We lost our finances, but as usual, my husband had an idea. *[With a touch of regret]* He thought he should tell Samarth the truth and ask him to marry a rich girl so we could bring some money into our home. Till that time, no one knew we were getting poorer day by day. *[Nostalgically]* When my son came to know about this, he was surprised but agreed to get married. Shimona is a very well-educated and rich woman. Her father thought we were rich too, hence he married her to my son. *[With a hint of sadness]* Later, he came to know about our condition, but Shimona was already married to my son by then. He became furious and asked her to leave my son, but she is a good lady; she told him she would never leave Samarth's side, even if he was poor. *[Resignedly]* We then had to sell our house. We came to live here in this wooden house, but Shimona struggled a lot and finally started her own company, after which money started coming in. *[Angrily]* My son was just like my husband. He never cared about her, only about money. He used to steal money from her account as well. *[With a hint of desperation]* My husband once met a priest who told him he could activate the necklace if Shimona was blessed with a baby boy. She got pregnant but delivered a baby girl. Both my husband and Samarth were furious and never accepted her, but just because Shimona was the only earning member of the family, she had the right to choose. *[Softly]* She told Samarth she would never give birth to any other child unless we accepted Amaira, her daughter. We agreed. Then, after two years, Sarthak was born.

**Ishan:** *[In disbelief]* But why did the necklace stop working?

**Ani Amma:** *[Nodding]* Oh yes, that. My son tried to find out everything he could about Adrian.

**Nisha:** *[Confused]* Who was Adrian?

**Ava:** *[Explaining]* The first guy who came to their house with a car, and Amma's husband killed him.

**Nisha:** *[Nodding]* Oh, yes, right.

**Ani Amma:** *[Tearfully]* Then he found out that Adrian had another wife, Devika, whom he had married secretly before marrying Roma. *[Pausing, with a hint of sorrow]* Because she was Hindu, he kept it a secret. Later, Devika had a daughter. After this, Adrian married Roma as his parents forced him to. *[With a pained expression]* Devika's daughter gave birth to a boy, years later. Because that boy was the descendant of Adrian, the necklace would only work if it were with him.

**Ani Amma:** *[Breaking down in tears]* My son killed that small boy in front of Devika and her daughter, Naina.

**Ishan:** *[Standing up and yelling]* What the hell is happening? Why aren't you all in jail? You and Shimona should also be in jail.

**Ani Amma:** *[Pleading]* No, son. Shimona does not know a thing about this. Please don't drag her into this. I am the one who should be in jail.

**Sash:** *[Comfortingly]* No Amma, you did nothing. You just happen to know about these things. You were not involved in any of those things.

**Ishan:** *[Bitterly]* Of course, one murderer will understand the other one better, right?

**Ani Amma:** *[Gently, holding Sayesha's hand]* Did you murder someone?

**Nisha:** *[Maturely]* No, Amma, she did not. That's a different story. She unintentionally killed a hamster who was Ishan's pet. So, he refers to her as a murderer.

Nisha handled everything very maturely. It started raining heavily, so Raghu closed all the doors and windows. It was cold, and everyone was hungry. Raghu had brought some food with him as he knew it was going to be a long night. Amma asked everyone if they wanted to eat dinner. They denied it as they were curious to know what happened next.

**Ishan:** *[Urgently]* Amma, what happened to that child's mother and Devika?

**Ani Amma:** *[Sadly]*, My son stole 10 crore rupees from Shimona's account and gave it to Devika and Naina to keep their mouths shut. *[Pausing, with sorrow]* Naina couldn't bear the wound and passed away after a few months. Naina's husband, Dhruv did not know anything about this because Samarth killed that boy while he was at Devika's house.

*[Reflectively]* Dhruv took care of Devika when she became old. She forced him to marry someone else, but he did not. Devika passed away four years back.

**Nisha:** *[Surprised]* Wow, you kept an eye on that family for so long.

**Ava:** *[Intrigued]* Did the necklace work again?

**Ani Amma:** *[Nodding]* When Sarthak was born, that priest did some ritual which made the necklace work but warned Samarth that in case any other male child is born in Adrian's family, this will stop working. So, we had to keep an eye on that family. *[Sighing]* Six months after Sarthak was born, we came to know that Shirley got married to a man named Ryan Xavier.

**Ava:** *[Excitedly]* No way. Ryan Xavier, that handsome famous businessperson who owns many multinational companies.

**Ani Amma:** *[Affirmatively]* Yes, that Ryan.

**Ava:** *[Enthusiastically]* He is, I guess, in his 50s and is so good-looking. When we were in college, he came as a guest speaker.

**Ishan:** *[Teasingly]* And you said you wanted to marry him.

**Ava:** *[Nostalgically]* Yes, my dream shattered when I found out he never wanted to get married.

**Nisha:** *[Dismissively]* As if he would have married you if he didn't say that.

**Ishan:** *[Irritated]* Girls, please. Do your gossips later. Let Amma talk first.

**Ani Amma:** *[Sentimentally]* I miss being with my friends. We used to gossip a lot. Okay then, when Shirley got pregnant, Samarth found out about it. *[With a hint of* *remorse]* He and my husband thought about how to find out the gender but couldn't come up with an idea.

Hence, when she was eight months pregnant, they made her car crash. *[Hesitantly]* She did not die on the spot, but labour pains started. We later found out that she died while giving birth, and her baby too.

**Ishan:** *[Shocked]* I can't believe it. The same thing happened with my mom, but I survived.

**Ani Amma:** *[Continuing]* When Xavier found out about this, he was devastated. *[With regret]* He was not that rich at the time. He just had a small company, but somehow, he managed to find out how the car crash happened. When he found out, he came to our house. *[With a hint of fear]* He didn't bring the police as he had no proof. He had a fight with my son and cursed our family, saying that every man in this family will die a painful death.

**Ishan:** *[Disbelieving]* And what happened next?

**Ani Amma:** *[Sadly]*, When Sarthak was five years old, my husband told him that we had a necklace which he needed to keep with him and pass on to future generations as it fulfilled all wishes. *[Regretfully]* Although Shimona was fulfilling all of Sarthak's wishes, his grandfather made him think it was because of the necklace.

**Ani Amma:** *[Explaining]* The necklace stopped working again after Shirley's death. When my husband went to see the priest, someone told him he had moved to Nepal. He couldn't find that priest again, so he tried all the mantras himself, but nothing worked. *[With a touch of despair]* My husband started becoming a maniac day by day as the necklace was not working. He used to sit all day in one room chanting mantras, doing some illogical stuff, and we were worried about his health. So, one day I told my son to tell him the necklace had started working and we were getting money because of it, as Shimona's work was not taking off. Only we knew the truth—that Shimona's business had taken off and we had become rich again. Logically, she became rich. Then we moved to our new house, where we are living now. *[With a tinge of nostalgia]* My husband was happy, and he thought it was all because of the necklace.

**Nisha:** *[Inquisitively]* Is it not visible in the necklace that it works or not? There should be some red or green light in the necklace indicating it is working.

**Ani Amma:** *[Shaking her head]* I saw that necklace only once when my husband stole it. After that, I have no idea how it works or not. Only the men of our family knew. *[With a sigh]* Later, my husband passed away in a road traffic accident, and it was a very painful death as cursed by Ryan. *[Pausing]* I distinctly remember, in the year 2000, my son came to know that Ryan's son was alive and to protect him from our family, he kept him in an orphanage.

**Ishan:** *[With tears in his eyes]* Really? This is how I find out Ryan is my father.

**Nisha:** *[Shocked]* Oh my god. Is Ryan Xavier your father? Remember, Ishan, you told us once you used to get anonymous gifts on your birthday when you were in the orphanage and that Aai used to tell you God loves you, so He sends you gifts every year.

**Ishan:** *[Nodding]* Yes... Now I know it was Dad. But those gifts stopped coming after I was 17 and left the orphanage.

**Ava:** *[Reassuringly]* Nope. The gifts still come. Remember, you told us when you were in college, you got a letter from a girl saying she liked you and wanted to keep her identity secret. We made fun of you, thinking it was fake, but then you got a gift from her on your birthday.

**Ishan:** *[Reflectively]* Oh yes, that girl. I still don't know her name and I still get gifts from her.

**Ava:** *[Realization dawning]* That's your dad.

**Nisha:** *[Disdainfully]* But he is very cheap then. Last year, he sent him that stupid used ring and bracelet after which we made fun of you.

**Ishan:** *[Smiling faintly]* He is not cheap. I now realize that it was my mom's belongings. But I don't understand one thing: he was not rich when my mom passed away, so he was scared that your son might want to kill me. But when he became one of the most powerful people in India, he could have easily accepted me.

**Ani Amma:** *[Sympathetically]* Son, parents are always worried for their children, no matter how rich or poor they are. Money can never buy any happiness or security. They are always scared to lose their kids. That's why he kept you low profile.

**Nisha:** *[Dismissively]* Oh please. He has so much security. We have seen that. Also, if he had told the truth to Ishan, he would never have told anyone.

**Ishan:** *[Contemplatively]* He might have been scared of how I would react and what if I told my friends who leak any information. But if he kept such a low profile, how did your son come to know about it?

**Ani Amma:** *[Hesitantly]* I don't know exactly how, but I do know he talked to a man on call who revealed this. He wanted to find you and kill you, but before he could do that, he died in the Bhuj earthquake in 2001.

**Nisha:** *[Inquiring]* What was he doing in Bhuj?

**Ishan:** *[Reflectively]* I went to Bhuj in 2001 with my friends for a trip when the massive earthquake came. We left from there just a day before. So, basically, he knew who I was, and he followed me.

**Ani Amma:** *[In awe]* Yes. God sees everything and He protected you all along. God killed Samarth.

**Ishan:** *[Determined]* No, my mother protected me.

**Ani Amma:** *[Apologetically]* Yes, my child. I am very sorry from my family for everything.

**Ishan:** *[Bitterly]* Sorry isn't enough. I used to cry so much and curse God on why He took away my parents. But it was all your family and not God. The reason for which was a stupid necklace.

**Ani Amma:** *[Solemnly]* Greed can turn a man into a monster, son.

**Ava:** *[Curiously]* How did Sarthak die, Amma?

**Ani Amma:** *[Soberly]* Sarthak hid the necklace after he came to know about his father's demise. He never knew all the money we had was all because of his mother and not that necklace. He met with an accident when he was drunk driving.

**Sash:** *[Understanding]* Then he chose me to find the necklace as he thought I was the one who sent police to his house.

**Ishan:** *[Convinced]* No, Sash. I think he knew I was the one who could activate that necklace; hence he chose to marry you and all that stupid stuff as he wanted to come close to me.

**Sash:** *[Puzzled]* Amma said he did not know this, Ishan. Why are you thinking like this?

**Ishan:** *[Pleading]* Amma, you did not tell us if you know the meaning of K.N.I.F.E.

**Ani Amma:** *[Shaking her head]* I do not know. We could never figure out.

**Nisha:** *[Directed to Raghu]* Raghu, you have been working in their family for a long time. You told us you were Sarthak's friend. Did you know anything about this?

*[Raghu was silent, looking down nervously. Ani Amma's eyes narrowed in anger.]*

**Ani Amma:** *[Demanding]* Raghuuu?? Do you know anything about this?

**Raghu:** *[Frightened]* Please leave me. I did not do anything. I am sorry.

**Ishan:** *[Intensely]* If you don't utter anything, I will beat you up.

**Raghu:** *[Desperate]* I will tell you everything. I knew this whole story. I am working in this family because I came to know about the necklace. I thought of stealing it, but then after working here, I came to know that it had stopped working. So, I tried everything I could to extract the truth.

**Ishan:** *[Inquiring]* Who told you about the necklace?

**Raghu:** *[Revealing]* My father was friends with Sarthak's grandfather, and as he became rich overnight, he knew something was going on. So, he called Kaka and asked him. Kaka did not reveal anything but tried to find the truth. Years later, he came to know about a necklace which makes wishes come true. So, he told me everything, and since then I started working here. Kaka did not know who I was, so he kept me as house help. I used to hide and listen to him, and Samarth talk, so I knew the whole thing. Kaka did not trust me at all, but one day I investigated myself and told him about Adrian's second wife. Since then, he started trusting me. I was the reason he came to know about Devika. I was the one who told him that Shirley was pregnant and that Shirley's son was alive. Anyhow, I wanted that necklace to work so that I could steal it. I too have a wife and two children. I wanted to see them grow and prosper.

**Ani Amma:** *[In shock]* You? I trusted you so much and you did all this? You were their secret agent? Whose son, are you?

**Raghu:** *[Timidly]* I am Rameshwar Prasad's son.

**Ani Amma:** *[Fuming]* That thief. I always hated him, but your Kaka loved him so much until he drifted apart from him when he started asking so many questions about how we became rich.

**Ishan:** *[Curious]* Did you tell anything to Sarthak?

**Raghu:** *[Nodding]* A few months before his death, I told Sarthak everything. He went in search of you but did not find a way to contact you. I told him to kill you so that the necklace would start working again, but Sarthak was not like his father. He did not have the guts to do that. So, we planned to be close to you and make you commit suicide.

**Ishan:** *[Horrified]* Suicide? How?

**Raghu:** *[Explaining]* Once, we followed you to a coffee shop where you and Kush were sitting. You told Kush how much you were in love with Sayesha, but she ignored you every time. One day, you saw her cry because her boss yelled at her, so you beat him up. You said, "I love Sash so much. I can never see her cry. I want to marry her." Then Kush said, "You are not her type. Don't be so obsessed with her. What will happen if she marries someone else?"

**Ishan:** *[Recalling]* I said I would die.

**Raghu:** *[Confirming]* Yes.

**Sash:** *[Shocked]* What?? You loved me? You were the reason my manager made me resign because you beat him up?

**Nisha:** *[Confused]* How come Ava and I never came to know about this?

**Ishan:** *[Apologetically]* I am sorry, Sash and Nisha. Some things are man-to-man talk, that's why. Raghu, continue the story.

**Raghu:** *[Reluctantly, revealing deeper secrets]* Then Sarthak planned on marrying Sayesha. He found out that Nisha's husband worked in his company and made him his friend. One day he called him, and when he was drunk, asked about Sayesha. Adesh revealed everything. Then they did all the stuff I told you earlier about Raj and all. *[In a deep voice]* He talked to Sayesha, and she refused to meet him. Then I told Sarthak to put her nudes on the internet, and when she was at her lowest, apologize to her and marry her.

**Ani Amma:** *[Disappointed and angry]* How terrible you are, Raghu. I had never expected you to do this to any woman. You have a daughter too.

**Raghu:** *[Ashamed and regretful]* I am sorry, really sorry. But Sarthak did not know Adesh would give Kush's number or that Kush's uncle was in CBI. All those things happened until Sarthak called Sayesha, who agreed to visit him. But later it turned out to be Kush and not Sayesha. He actually planned to ask her to marry him but did not know what was going to happen. *[Raghu explains how Sarthak's plans failed due to unforeseen complications.]* He was very angry that day, so he planned on murdering Sayesha. He was not this type, but rejection hurt him. Moreover, he was furious to see Kush, rather than Sayesha. He went to a tantric to ask for help to get rid of her. The tantric refused at first, but then Sarthak promised him lots of money. So, the tantric told him he could make her soul reach another world where it would be impossible to return from. Sarthak just had to bring her to his place anyhow. Sarthak agreed to do that. He thought he would let Sayesha know somehow that Raj had committed suicide after a girl rejected him and then haunt her in the name of Raj. When she was scared, he would slip the tantric's address to her, telling her...

**Sash:** *[Shocked and hurt]* To trade my soul if I wanted his help to...

**Ishan:** *[Realizing]* Remove Raj's soul from her life.

**Raghu:** *[Revealing with a mix of guilt and detachment]* When Kush and Ishan came to our building, I told Sarthak to kill Ishan then and there but due to Sayesha's betrayal his purpose changed from killing Ishan to killing Sayesha. He thought if Sayesha died, Ishan would automatically kill himself.

**Ishan:** *[Disbelieving]* I was young, and everyone says such things like "I would die if she married someone else" and blah blah. Sarthak was so lame. How did he think I would actually die?

**Raghu:** *[Reflective and regretful]* He was not lame but innocent. I told him you would not die, but he did not understand that. *[Raghu acknowledges Sarthak's naivety and his own failure to guide him correctly.]* It was easy to convince him most of the time, but in this case, I tried a lot, but he did not listen at all. *[Frustated]* He even hid the necklace without telling me where he kept it. That day after meeting the tantric, he was very happy and got drunk. He should not have done that as he met with an accident and passed away.

When he died, I tried to find the necklace but then lost hope. A few months later, Sayesha came to visit Shimona madam. I heard whatever she said, so I understood Sarthak's plan was in place even after he died. The only difference was he wanted to kill Raj, but he died in real.

By coincidence, I went to the Hanuman temple with my wife where I saw Sayesha crying. I thanked God as I thought He was with me. I told my wife to talk to her and take her to that tantric. I went to the tantric's place and told him the plan continues. I would give him the money. I even transferred one lakh to him. Sayesha did not know, but I was there when she reached. I was hiding in the other room.

She ruined my plan after she brought Hari to trade souls. The tantric had no other option but to do the rituals, and he was sure Hari would come back, but unknowingly something happened, and Hari got stuck there, maybe because he was old and weak. When Hari died, the tantric got a paralysis attack, and many bad things happened at his place. He was furious.

We tried to contact Sayesha after that and told her she would have to apologize to Hari and gave her one month's time. I thought in a month, I would find the necklace. I even found a necklace that looked exactly like Kaka described it. I was happy and waiting for Sayesha to go back to the tantric.

One night, the tantric called me and told me Sayesha and Ishan, along with some other friends, were at his place. *[Smirking]* I told him to send both to the other world, and in this way, both would die, fulfilling Sarthak's wish and mine too. The necklace would get activated once Ishan died. I would leave with the necklace.

He started the ritual, but something happened that we had never thought of. Sayesha met Hari, brought him back, and both Sayesha and Ishan came back alive. *[Frustration evident from his face].* The tantric could not believe it. He called me and told me everything. He said he had never seen anyone come back alive from that place, but some miracle had happened, and now he could not help me. He was shocked as he had not even told you the way back to this universe. He also told me you were in search of that necklace.

I knew Sayesha always had in her mind why Sarthak chose her, so when you all came to talk to Shimona mam, I told you that story but only lied about one thing: that I was not involved in it.

**Ishan:** *[Demanding answers]* Answer me these questions—Sarthak is dead, right?

**Raghu:** *[Confirming]* Yes.

**Ishan:** *[Intensely]* He wanted me and Sayesha dead.

**Raghu:** *[Nodding]* Yes.

**Ishan:** *[Grimly]* Sarthak is haunting Sash in real?

**Raghu:** *[Uneasy]* Yes, he is haunting her in real, and I have no idea how. I just know that spirits come to earth for some unfinished business.

**Ishan:** *[Pressing further]* Sarthak told Sayesha someone has made his father and grandfather captive. Who is he?

**Raghu:** *[Confused and defensive]* I don't know, Sir.

**Ishan:** *[Demanding]* If I touch the necklace, will it get activated?

**Raghu:** *[Reluctantly]* Yes, as far as I know.

**Ishan:** *[Determined]* Where is the necklace?

**Raghu:** *[Defiantly]* I have it with me.

**Ishan:** *[Questioning]* Why did you bring Amma here tonight?

**Raghu:** *[Explaining]* I did not bring her. She told me to drop her. I just insisted I stay as I thought I might kill you tonight, but...

**Ishan:** *[Realizing]* Amma revealed everything, and I pulled you, so you got scared.

**Raghu:** *[Admitting]* Yes.

**Ishan:** *[Mocking]* Hahaha... Bullshit. I know you still have a plan. I just don't know why you told us the truth. Maybe because it's better to tell the dying person the truth?

**Ava:** *[Panic-stricken]* Wait, Ishan. I must go to the washroom now. Please. I cannot control it.

**Ishan:** *[Firmly]* Okay, you go. I will handle this, Raghu.

**Raghu:** *[Desperately]* No, I do not have any plan.

**Ishan:** *[Determined]* Nisha, throw all the food Raghu got with him. It is poisoned.

When Nisha was about to get up, Raghu pushed Ishan and tried to run away. Ishan hit him with a tin box lying there, and Raghu got hurt in his head. Sayesha at once emptied the polybag which had food and wrapped Raghu's head with it. Ishan pulled his leg, and he fell on the ground. Amma gave them her dupatta to tie him up. Nisha tied the dupatta onto his hands, and they made him sit on a chair. They then rolled a bedsheet and tied Raghu to the chair. Ishan then removed the polybag from Raghu's face and asked:

**Ishan:** *[Demanding]* Where is the necklace?

**Raghu:** *[Defiantly]* I will not tell you anything.

**Sayesha:** *[Disturbed, angry] [Slaps him] [Trying to calm herself]* Ishan, let me sit down.

**Ishan:** *[Calmly]* Nisha, please check his bag. Nisha checked the bag and did not find anything.

**Nisha:** *[Worried]* What is Ava doing inside the washroom for so long? *[Shouting]* Ava... Ava...

**Ava:** *[Nonchalantly]* Coming...

**Nisha:** *[Irritated]* What were you doing inside for so long?

**Ava:** *[Defensive]* Really? Do you think I need to answer this question? Oh my god, why is Raghu all tied up?

Nisha explained everything to Ava. Ava got an idea. She pulled down Raghu's pants.

**Sash:** *[Shocked]* What the hell are you doing, Ava?

**Ava:** *[Urgently]* Shut up, Sash.... Ishan, put your hand inside his underwear.

**Ishan:** *[Confused]* Are you crazy?

**Ava:** *[Confidently]* The necklace is in there.

**Raghu:** *[Desperate]* Don't you dare touch it.

When Raghu said this, Ishan realized that Ava was right. All of them turned their faces in the opposite direction when Ishan pulled out the necklace from his underwear.

**Ishan:** *[Triumphantly]* You all can turn around. I found the necklace. Wow, Ava, how did you know that?

**Ava:** *[Proudly]* Well, I watch a lot of crime shows. When people can hide weed, then he can hide a necklace as well. The necklace was so dear to him, it was impossible he would have left it somewhere else. I was sure the necklace was with him, and when I removed his pants, I saw something shiny inside his underwear. Of course, nothing else shines there. *[Winks]*

She winked. All of them had a great laugh.

**Raghu:** *[Frustrated]* What are you all going to do with me now? Kill me?

**Ava:** *[Calmly]* No, Raghu Bhaiya. You just wait and watch.

**Ishan:** *[Whispering to Ava]* I have no plan. Do you think we should call the police?

**Ava:** *[Reassuringly]* Chill... I already did call someone.

**Ani Amma:** *[Demanding]* Show me the necklace.

Ishan cleaned the necklace and handed it over to Amma.

**Ani Amma:** *[Shocked]* This is my necklace. This is not some magical necklace. I have worn it multiple times. Samarth gifted me this on my birthday.

**Ishan:** *[Confused]* But Amma, it would have been possible that he gave you the real necklace.

**Amma:** *[Firmly]* I have seen the real necklace, stupid boy. This isn't it. Also, females are not allowed to touch the real necklace, so why would he give it to me?

Nisha started laughing and said, "We made him remove his pants for a fake necklace."

**Raghu:** *[Perplexed]* If this isn't the necklace, then why was it wrapped in a cloth which said, "This is the secret gift."

**Ani Amma:** *[Smiling, reminiscing]* Oh, that. When Samarth was small, he used to gift me things on my birthday like some handmade things, a pen, a card, etc., and always used to tell me this is the secret gift. This was his thing, so when he had this necklace made for me, he covered it with a muslin cloth and got that line engraved with thread. You were also there when he gifted me this.

**Raghu:** *[Trying to recall]* I don't remember. I just remember Sarthak telling me that the necklace has crystals like ruby, emerald, and pearl. So, I thought this was it.

Suddenly there was a knock on the door. When Nisha opened, she saw Ryan Xavier standing outside. When he saw Ishan, his eyes filled with tears. Before he could say anything, Ishan hugged him and said:

**Ishan:** *[Emotionally]* Thank you for coming, DAD.

This was the first time Ryan heard "DAD" from Ishan's mouth. He was thrilled and emotional simultaneously.

**Ryan:** *[Softly]* I am sorry, Son. You had to find out the things in this way. I always wanted to keep you with me, but you weren't safe here. Hence, I left you at the orphanage.

**Ishan:** *[Understandingly]* I know everything. I can understand. Just promise me you won't leave me now.

**Ryan:** *[Sincerely]* I promise.

**Ishan:** *[Curiously]* But how did you know I was here?

**Ryan:** *[Smiling]* Ava told me.

**Ishan:** *[Incredulously]* Ava, how did you have his number? Please, no more mysteries.

**Ava:** *[Explaining]* I told you earlier that he came to our college as a guest speaker. He gave us a number in case we needed any help in the future—his business number of course *[raising her eyebrows]*. I always wanted to call that number but never did. When you were talking to Raghu, I knew something was going to happen, so I went to the washroom to dial his number, but there was waiting.

Finally, a guy picked up, and I asked to speak to Ryan. He said he doesn't talk to everyone and asked for the reason. I told him his son was on the verge of death. After 5 minutes, Ryan called me, and I told him a few things and gave him this address.

**Ishan:** *[Gratefully]* Thank you, Ava.

**Nisha:** *[Noticing]* Why is Sash so quiet?

**Sash:** *[Distantly]* No, nothing.

**Ishan:** *[Concerned]* Is there anything else, Sash?

**Sash:** *[Hesitantly]* No, I was wondering where the real necklace is.

**Ishan:** *[Dismissively]* It doesn't matter. I do not care at all. I just know I found my dad and will meet my real family soon.

**Sash:** *[Worried]* But what about Sarthak? Will he stop haunting me, and who is that man who has held his father and grandfather captive? He still has not gotten what he wanted. Will he come back for us? Was our interpretation of K.N.I.F.E. right?

**Ishan:** *[Resolutely]* We will think about it.

No one else uttered a single word. After some time, the police arrived. They caught Raghu and Mrs. Anindita for their crimes. Ava and Nisha were very tired. All of them decided to go to the hospital to meet Kush as the mystery was solved, and the necklace was still at an unknown place. Without Ishan, the necklace would never get activated, hence it was not of any harm.

They locked the safe house, and this time Ishan drove back to the hospital with his dad while Ava drove the other car. Sayesha was still in a double mind. They reached the hospital to meet Kush and she got out of the car.

Sayesha turned around, her heart pounding as she noticed a figure seated on a bench near the graveyard. Struggling to see clearly through the dim light, she inched closer, drawn by an unsettling sense of anxiety. As she approached, the man on the bench slowly turned his face towards her, and the world seemed to freeze.

Her breath caught in her throat as she recognized him. It was Sarthak, wearing the necklace with a chilling, malevolent smile.

The night seemed to grow darker around him, making his smile even more frightening. Sayesha was frozen in place, overwhelmed by a cold, terrifying feeling.

# THE END

## Author's Bio

Dr. Shubhada Chourishi is a dynamic professional blending expertise in medicine and psychology. Originally from Ratlam, Madhya Pradesh, she holds an MBBS degree from MUHS Nashik and pursued MD in Emergency Medicine Services, complemented by a Fellowship in Psychology. Dr. Shubhada practices in Pune, where she runs her own clinic, Nirvaan Healthcare Clinic, specializing in outpatient care and therapeutic interventions such as Cognitive Behavioural Therapy *(CBT)* and Neuro-Linguistic Programming *(NLP)*.

Known for her in-depth knowledge of face reading in behavioural genetics, she is also a certified life coach, guiding individuals towards personal growth and fulfilment.

Beyond her professional endeavours, she enjoys a diverse range of hobbies including reading, writing, painting, drawing, and singing. She excels as a speaker and anchor, captivating audiences with her engaging presence. A passionate advocate for mental health, she engages in discussions and initiatives aimed at promoting well-being. A dedicated dog lover, she shares her life with two beloved furry companions.

An ardent fan of Harry Potter, Dr. Shubhada believes in finding happiness in life's simple pleasures and strives to inspire others through her work and personal philosophy. Known for her positivity, self-motivation, and infectious enthusiasm, she embraces life with a zest for living.

www.ingramcontent.com/pod-product-compliance
Lightning Source LLC
LaVergne TN
LVHW061615070526
838199LV00078B/7292